I0761864

Seaside Haven

Seaside Haven

Book 1 in the Seaside Series

Sandra W. Burch

Seaside Haven

Published by Revival Waves of Glory Books & Publishing

PO Box 596| Litchfield, Illinois 62056 USA

www.revivalwavesofgloryministries.com

Revival Waves of Glory Books & Publishing is committed to excellence in the publishing industry.

Published in the United States of America

EBook: 978-1-329-01579-1

Paperback: 978-1-329-01577-7

Hardcover: 978-1-329-01578-4

Table of Contents

Jeremiah 29:11 "For I know the plans I have for you," declares the LORD, "plans to prosper you and not to harm you, plans to give you hope and a future."

Chapter One

Thunder rolled overhead as rain spat like gunfire on Seaside's sandy beachfront. Mother Nature's fury, however, was no match for the emotions churning inside Sierra Ramstad. Unmindful of the storm, she continued to walk. In the pocket of the red raincoat she wore, she fisted her slender hand around the crumpled piece of paper and recalled its content.

Miss Ramstad:

I will be arriving home tomorrow for an extended stay. Please have my room ready.

- Phoenix Chamberlain

Two curt sentences that had her blood boiling.

Phoenix Chamberlain, III, heir to the Chamberlain fortune, was coming home, as he'd put it, to recuperate after the car accident he'd been involved in three months earlier.

If the news reports she'd read about his accident was even remotely accurate, then Sierra supposed she should feel sorry for him. Along with a concussion and a dislocated shoulder, he'd broken his ankle and shattered the femur in his left leg. Three months out and the man was in the midst of a long and painful recovery. Even so she didn't want him mending here, and possibly meddling in the day-to-day operations of Seaside Haven Resort.

Phoenix's family had a large home outside of Atlanta, Georgia, as well as an assortment of plush real estate sprinkled around Europe. Why hadn't he picked one of those places to recuperate? Surely they would be more accommodating to Phoenix's entourage who enabled his larger-than-life existence.

Why choose Seaside Haven? This wasn't his home. It was *hers*! While Phoenix had spent the past few years jet setting around Europe, living off a sizable trust fund and enjoying the life of the rich and famous, Sierra had been working to turn an old and nearly forgotten inn into a resort that offered five-star accommodations, panoramic views, and above all, excellent service.

Now Phoenix was returning and he wanted his room readied. It was Sierra's understanding that he hadn't visited the resort since his childhood. So she'd made the owner's private room on the main floor her own, and turned the adjacent apartment into a luxury suite that commanded a substantial sum of money to occupy it.

Muttering words that were muffled by the wind, she stopped and looked back in the direction she had come. The cedar shingled resort stood four stories tall, given the pilings that raised it above sea level to protect it from flooding. Her gaze skimmed the balconies that stretched out from each room to maximize the view. Even though it was early afternoon, the lights burned brightly in the windows of guests waiting out the storm.

Home.

Phoenix might refer to it as such, but for Sierra it truly was her home. It was here she'd come after her nasty divorce. The warm sunshine and the sense of purpose had ushered her back from the brink of despair.

With a reluctant sigh, Sierra headed back. Other guests would be arriving soon and that meant she had a job to do. Right now, her priority was to see that all new arrivals were settled in their rooms. Once that task was completed, she'd figure out her own accommodations for the duration of Phoenix's stay.

By the time she reached the resort, any part of her body that wasn't covered by the raincoat was drenched. She had hoped to have enough time to change into dry clothes and do something with her hair before any guests arrived, but a pearl white Cadillac Escalade with dark tinted windows was pulling up at the main entrance as she came around the sand dune.

The driver hopped out, as did another man who came around from the passenger side. Both were big and robust. It wasn't a surprise to see bodyguards as a lot of the resort's guests were Hollywood A-listers or business moguls. Before either man could reach the handle, the rear driver side door swung open.

Sierra covered her mouth with the palm of her hand, but a gasp still escaped.

Phoenix Chamberlain, III.

She had never met him in person. They had exchanged emails a couple of times a month, and occasionally a phone call. But he'd never come for a visit. Now here he was. And he wasn't at all what Sierra had expected.

Every photograph she had seen of him on social media showed a handsome young man with wavy, black hair, deep set dark brown eyes, a carefree smile and a body toned to perfection under the capable tutelage of a well-paid professional trainer.

Meanwhile, the man trying to exit the SUV's rear seat was thin and fragile. The dark smudges under his eyes made it clear that he hadn't been getting much sleep despite many hours spent in bed. And his rigid posture and pinched features indicated he was far from carefree.

"I'll get the wheelchair, Mr. Chamberlain," said the man who'd come around from the front passenger side.

"No! I'll walk," he snapped in an angry rasp that carried over the howling wind.

"But, Mr. Chamberlain…" the driver began, only to be shouted down.

"I said I'll walk, Tommy! I'm not an invalid!"

Phoenix had to use his hands to manipulate his left leg over the threshold. He swung his right leg out the door without much effort. Then, lowering himself to the running board, he eased his feet to the ground. He held a cane in one hand and used the other to grip the door frame. Unfortunately, neither support was enough. A mere second after both of his feet were on the pavement, his left knee buckled. The man he'd called Tommy caught Phoenix under his arms before he hit the pavement. Loud cursing followed. The other man rushed forward, as did Sierra, determined to help.

"Who are you?" Phoenix barked, shaking off the hand that she had placed on his arm.

She pushed back the hood of the raincoat and offered what she hoped was a pleasant and professional smile. Despite the raincoat's hood, her golden blond hair was damp and her bangs were plastered against her forehead. As for makeup, she doubted what she'd applied that morning still lingered on her eyes and cheeks now. Her feet were bare and spattered with wet sand. It was hardly the image she'd planned to portray when she first met him.

"I'm Sierra Ramstad."

Phoenix continued to stare at her as if she were something to be studied under a microscope.

"We've spoken on the phone and via email for several years now. I manage Seaside Haven."

"Of course you do." His gaze flickered down in seeming dismissal. Although he said it under his breath, she heard him when he added, "I had you pegged right."

So, he had preconceived notions of her, did he? That didn't come as a surprise. She had entertained plenty of her own where he was concerned. Still, it made her mad that, after a glance, he could marginalize her personally and probably professionally.

Sierra cleared her throat and drew herself up to her full height of five foot five. Since Phoenix was hunched over, it put them at eye level. When their eyes met she didn't as much as blink. Using her most professional tone, she told him, "I wasn't expecting you until tomorrow."

"I changed my mind."

"That's obvious!"

"I was in Atlanta visiting my mom…" His words trailed off and his expression hardened. "I'm here now. I trust that is not a problem, Miss Ramstad."

"No problem," she assured him with a stiff smile. "I just need to explain that your room isn't ready."

"Am I to wait out here until it is?" he questioned irritably.

Standing under the portico, they were protected from the worst of the storm, but the wind blew sideways splattering them with rain every now and again.

"Oh, of course not," she replied as heat crept into her face. She turned on her heel and walked toward the lobby entrance, calling over her left shoulder, "Right this way, gentlemen."

Phoenix allowed Tommy and Adam to assist him in the direction of the door. Another time, he would have felt bad about the way he'd talked to her. But unfortunately for her, both his usual good humor and his playboy charm was like his leg; fractured beyond repair. Or so the physicians said. But they were wrong. They had to be. He couldn't spend the rest of his life this way.

The doors opened announcing their arrival. The lobby looked different than he remembered from the last time Phoenix had been to Seaside Haven. Varying shades of blue and yellow dominated the color scheme, accentuated with white and a shade of tan that reminded Phoenix of sand. The glow of the table lamps gave the room a warm, welcoming ambiance despite the storm that raged outside.

He exhaled slowly and some of the tension left his neck and shoulders. He was a long way from relaxed but Phoenix knew he had made the right decision to come here.

He glanced around the room again. "This is really nice," he said to no one in particular.

"The remodeling was completed this spring. All of the rooms have been updated in a similar color scheme." Sierra cleared her throat. Her tone was almost defensive when she added, "I emailed you numerous photographs."

Truth be known, he probably hadn't opened the email attachments. He was too busy spending his trust fund to care, he thought with a mental grimace.

"Well, the photographs didn't do it justice," he exclaimed.

Nor, Phoenix admitted to himself, had the image he'd had of Sierra done her justice.

For the past few years, he'd signed her paychecks, skimmed over the monthly reports, and approved her capital investments all the while offering minimal input. He'd never laid eyes on the woman he'd entrusted his resort to. Until now.

Sierra had shed the raincoat and stood in front of the reception desk wearing a blue polo shirt adorned with the resort's logo and a pair of white shorts that stopped mid-thigh. Her legs were tanned and toned. Phoenix's gaze lifted to her small waist before rising to her breasts, which were just the right size to fill his hands.

He tore his gaze away from her, surprised he was gawking the woman as if he were a sex-crazed frat boy on spring break. At the same time, he was relieved by his reaction, as he'd felt dead for far too long.

"If you don't mind, I need to get off of my feet, Miss Ramstad." Pain turned his tone gruff.

"Yes, of course, Mr. Chamberlain." She gave a curt nod. "Please, follow me."

Pride demanded that he do so under his own power. No matter how slow that would make the going.

"Adam, help Tommy with my bags."

Adam Vinateri had been his personal trainer, now he worked as his physical therapist. But he didn't mind lending a hand when called on to do so. After all, he was paid well for little work since Phoenix regularly skipped his daily stretching and strengthening exercises.

Phoenix knew he needed to do the exercises. But knowing and doing them were two different things. Most days, he didn't bother to get out of bed, because physician after physician offered such a grim prognosis.

He shifted his weight from his good leg to his bad one. The pain was excruciating and he bit back a groan, wondering if it had been wise to swear off the narcotics the doctor prescribed. The pain pills made him feel brain dead and he was afraid that the state of oblivion might prove to be addictive.

His progress was slow and his gait uneven but at least he was walking on his own. Sierra turned around once, concern obvious in her expression, but she didn't offer any assistance. Apparently, his rude dismissal of her help had done the trick. And for that he was glad. Phoenix hated the way people treated him like an invalid.

Women had been among the worst offenders. That was one of the reasons he'd dissed the entourage of females that accompanied him at the chalet. As for his male friends, the number had dwindled substantially once it became obvious Phoenix no longer would be throwing any of the parties for which he had been known for.

Users, every last one of them. What did that say about him, Phoenix wondered? The only loyalty he commanded was among people such as Tommy and Adam and of course, Miss Ramstad, all of whom were on his payroll.

Behind the reception desk, a door led to a hallway. To the left were the business office and supply room. Phoenix remembered playing hide-and-seek in them when he visited his grandfather. The owner's bedroom was on the right. The door was closed and the word PRIVATE was engraved on a plaque affixed just below the peephole. After Sierra pulled a key from her pocket and opened it, Phoenix stepped over the threshold, expecting to be assailed with memories of his grandfather, the one person in his life whose love had been unconditional. But as in the lobby, nothing was as he remembered. Given his emotional state, he wasn't sure whether he was grateful for that or not.

The last time Phoenix had been inside of the room, the décor had been more masculine. It wasn't only the pale shade of paint on the wall, and the furnishings that made it seem feminine, it was the smell. The scent that lingered in the air was not that of his grandfather's Swisher Sweet cigars. Rather, it was a light and fresh scent. Her scent. He inhaled deeply, finding it comforting and arousing at the same time. He shoved the thought aside, only to have another take its place.

"Do you stay in here?"

Sierra frowned. "Yes, for the past few years. Room and board are one of the perks of the manager's job."

"I know that! But this room was my grandfathers. It is for the owner, Miss Ramstad."

Her tone was as incredulous as her expression. "But I told you…"

Phoenix cut her off. "I thought there was an adjacent room to accommodate the manager."

Sierra's mouth puckered at his statement, drawing Phoenix's attention to her plump lips that needed no added color to make them appealing.

"There is, or rather, there was. But since this room was empty all the time, I...that is, *we* decided it made more sense to turn the adjacent manager's room into a luxurious suite that could accommodate guests for an extended stay."

"*We* did?" Phoenix questioned.

Color rose in her cheeks. "I sent you several cost-benefit analysis reports and you said that you agreed with my suggestions."

"I remember now." Phoenix nodded, although he was damned if he could recall doing any such thing.

Every dime Sierra had invested in the resort had paid off, he decided. Whereas he had been reckless in the past, the risks she'd taken had been calculated and well planned. He might have approved her plans, but the ideas had been hers alone. Although Phoenix had a degree in Marketing and Management, one that he'd never had to use, he would be wise to learn from his very competent manager, Miss Ramstad.

"It's been full ever since," she chimed.

Which meant it was full now.

Phoenix appreciated her ability to turn unused space into a profitable one, but it did make for an awkward situation. He couldn't hold out any longer. "Where are you going to sleep, Miss Ramstad?"

Where was *she* going to sleep?

Sierra gritted her teeth and offered what she hoped passed for an unconcerned smile.

"I'll figure out something for the duration of your stay." As unspecified as that might be.

Phoenix staggered to the sofa and dropped heavily onto the plush cushions, his face drawn with a grimace. Sheer will power had kept him upright, of that she was certain. She might have admired his tenacity if it weren't accompanied by such a brusque disposition.

"Well, there must be at least one available guest room, right?" For the first time, he sounded more uncertain than he did ornery.

"No, we're full." She exhaled slowly. "Actually, we're booked for the rest of the season barring any last-minute cancellations." When Phoenix continued to gawk at her, she added, "It's been an excellent summer so far. Revenues are up by…"

He cut her off abruptly. "Well, you can't sleep in the lobby, Miss Ramstad!"

Sierra had made the same determination, but her options were limited. The only alternative was…

Her gaze cut to the adjacent room where she exercised when the weather prevented her from walking on the beach. It had a futon that made into what her twin sister, Sienna, claimed was a comfortable bed. Her sister was the only overnight guest Sierra had entertained. On a sigh, she recalled her upcoming visit. She'd have to let her know plans had changed. Yet another disruption in her well-organized schedule.

"I'll stay in the exercise room," she said at last.

"No!" His tone made the single syllable sound final.

Sierra felt her blood pressure rise. The man certainly knew how to push her buttons. She didn't like being told what to do. Since her divorce, no man had dared, nor would she have tolerated it. She had a voice and these days she used it with impunity.

"It will be a tight fit," she admitted. Not to mention that she would have to figure out where to shower and stow her clothes, but at least it offered her more privacy than the resort's common areas.

Phoenix leaned his head back on the sofa and closed his eyes. Dressed in all black, a color that mirrored his mood, she couldn't help but notice how out of place he looked amid the array of colorful throw pillows. The taut line of his mouth and the way his brow creased made it clear that he was in pain.

"When was the last time you took a pain pill?" she quizzed. She tried to keep her tone neutral, careful to keep any concern from seeping into it.

"I quit those a few weeks ago," he mumbled. Just when she started to think that his decision stemmed from some macho man bull, he added, "They make me feel brain dead. The last thing I need is to become addicted to pain killers."

His reasoning was sound, even though his pain was left unmanaged.

The two men who accompanied Phoenix strode into the room. The driver was tugging a pair of suitcases that were large enough to hold Sierra's entire wardrobe. The other man pushed the wheelchair. A smaller bag was nestled on its seat with a garment bag draped over top of it. Sierra's stomach knotted. Phoenix had brought a lot of baggage, in more ways than one.

"Where do you want your things, Mr. Chamberlain?" the driver asked.

Without opening his eyes, Phoenix motioned with one hand in the direction of the closet. "Put them in there, Tommy."

"And mine, boss?" asked the guy pushing the wheelchair.

Phoenix did open his eyes now as he straightened in his seat. "I guess you will be here on the sofa, Adam. Since Miss Ramstad will be in the adjacent room."

Chapter Two

Phoenix waved a hand. "Not to be rude, but if you could move your belongings out of my room and be on your way, I'd appreciate it very much. I need to lie down."

He didn't wait for her to respond. He turned his head on the pillow and closed his eyes.

Sierra had been dismissed like the hired help she was. And his dismissal made her blood boil once more. It took an effort, but she managed to swallow her pride. "Sure, Mr. Chamberlain, I'd be happy to oblige."

Although the rooms were neat, she would have to change the linens on the bed before Phoenix used it. She'd planned to do that chore in the morning, as well as gather up her clothes and toiletries in anticipation of his arrival. But showing up early, and bringing other guests had left her feeling inadequate.

When the driver exited the room, Sierra stepped into the adjacent doorway. Glancing around the room, she tapped a finger to her lips. The treadmill would have to be moved to the corner of the room in order to open the futon bed, which would also need clean linens. Same for the bedroom's pullout sofa, where Phoenix had assigned his therapist, Adam, to bunk.

As if reading her mind, Adam said from behind her, "I'm sorry for all of the inconvenience our stay is causing you."

Sierra turned, taking in his sweet smile. She guessed him to be a few years younger than her, which would put him in his early twenties. Despite his age, his face was almost boyish.

"It's no problem," she lied.

He let go of one of the wheelchair handles and extended his hand. "I'm Adam Vinateri."

"I'm Sierra Ramstad. It's nice to meet you, Adam."

He nodded. "Would it be okay if I kept my things in this room?

Sierra nodded and pointed across the room to a dresser. "If you'd like, you can put some of your things in there. And there's plenty of room in the closet if you need to hang up your clothes."

"Thanks. But I'm t-shirt and shorts kind of guy."

She nearly smiled.

Adam's simple wardrobe explained his medium sized suitcase while his boss had brought a pair of large suitcases as well as a garment bag. The designer labeled clothing inside of the bags wasn't the issue. The amount of clothing stated he was planning a far more extended stay than she'd assumed.

"This is a nightmare," Sierra muttered, momentarily forgetting about Adam.

"It's okay." Not surprisingly, Adam misunderstood what she meant and gave her a reassuring smile. Then motioning over his shoulder, he added, "He's not so bad, once you get to know him."

"I'm sure." Her attempt at sounding convincing fell far from short.

"Mr. Chamberlain is in a lot of pain right now," he insisted.

She nodded. "Phoenix told me he's not taking the pain medication that the doctors prescribed."

Adam leaned in closer and dropped his voice to barely above a whisper. "The accident has taken an emotional toll as well, although I doubt he'd admit it."

Sierra supposed she shouldn't find that surprising. Even the strongest people could succumb to depression.

"How bad is his injury?"

"Well, to be honest Ms. Ramstad, it's one of the worst I've seen. Major ligament damage in addition to the bone fractures. The doctors advised amputating it above the knee." Adam shook his head as he exhaled.

"Oh, my God!" Sierra gasped. "I had no idea it was so severe."

"Yes, he managed to keep that from being leaked to the press. His *friends*..." Adam snorted, as if finding the word laughable. "They provided information and photographs to the press. Mr. Chamberlain was not happy about it."

"Sounds like he needs a better class of friends!"

Adam nodded at her assessment. "I was delighted when he announced we would be returning to Florida. Some of his friends probably haven't noticed he's gone, although they'll get the picture when the chalet is sold."

Sierra's jaw dropped. "Sold?"

"Phoenix has made it clear that he doesn't want to go back there. Of course, it might be the depression doing the talking."

One could hope. Because if he didn't go back there, she had a sickening feeling he might stay here.

"How's his therapy going?" she asked, hoping for good news.

But that wasn't what she got.

"Slow." Adam sighed. "Since most days he doesn't want to do his exercises."

"That must make your job difficult."

"Oh, it does. And it feeds his frustration, as well, because he refuses to give up hope."

"Of walking without a cane?" Sierra inquired.

Adam nodded. "Walking without a cane…running…. skiing. He wants to be as good as before the accident."

"That's not likely to happen, is it?" she asked softly.

Adam cleared his throat. "I have already said too much, Miss Ramstad. I just wanted you to know why he is being a jerk."

"I understand. Thanks."

When Sierra returned to her bedroom, Phoenix's large suitcases were open on the foot of the bed.

"I'll need a bureau where I can put away his things. Hope you can accommodate me, Miss Ramstad."

Where Phoenix barked orders, his employees asked politely. She appreciated their manners.

"Sure." She grabbed a tote bag from the closet and started to fill it with her things. Over her shoulder, she called out, "I'll be out of your way in a few minutes."

"Oh, no rush, Miss Ramstad."

"Please, call me Sierra."

Adam smiled.

While she finished filling her bag with clothes, he hung an assortment of designer clothing in the closet. All of the garments screamed expensive and were far more formal than the t-shirt and shorts Adam had on. Did Phoenix plan to wear them? If so, when and where? Once again, she had an uneasy feeling that her employer was here for the long haul.

Phoenix Chamberlain was accustomed to a robust social life, if the press images were to be believed. Of course, that was before his car accident. Recently, the only time his photograph had graced the tabloids, his palms had been up, as if to ward off the swarming paparazzi, and he'd worn the same pain-induced grimace she'd seen firsthand.

Sierra finished clearing out the bureau and hastily grabbed a section of outfits from the closet, which she took to the adjacent room. Adam had finished unpacking his suitcase and was glancing around.

"Can I help you with something?" Sierra asked.

"I've got some equipment that I need to bring in for Mr. Chamberlain's sessions. I don't think you want it in the lobby."

He was right about that. "The resort has a gym on the main floor. There should be room in there for your equipment."

"Mr. Chamberlain has to have privacy."

Sierra nodded. She couldn't blame him for that. "If I have my treadmill moved to storage, will that be enough space?"

Adam squinted, as if visualizing the room sans the item she had mentioned. "Yes, I think that will work."

"Great! I'll call someone to move it."

"No need. Tommy and I can handle it."

"All right." That was settled. The invasion of her privacy was officially complete.

She forced a smile that was cut short by a snuffle coming from Phoenix. "Can the two of you skip the chitchat? I know that you have more things to do with your time than flirt!" he yelled.

Flirt? Sierra felt her face turn red, but it wasn't merely embarrassment that brought the heat rushing into her cheeks. The nerve of the man accusing her of flirting, as if spending a few minutes talking to a colleague meant she was interested in him. And to think minutes earlier she had started to feel sorry for Phoenix. Every ounce of empathy had evaporated now.

Adam nodded. "Sorry, Mr. Chamberlain," he mouthed.

Sierra nodded but she was too mad to say she was sorry.

While Adam and Tommy moved the treadmill to storage to make room for the physical therapy equipment, she changed the linens on the futon bed where she would sleep, gathered up her toiletries from the bathroom and put out clean towels. Then, satisfied that everything was in order, she turned to leave.

As Sierra entered the bedroom, she braced herself for an unpleasant exchange. But to her surprise, Phoenix was asleep on the sofa. His bad leg was propped on the coffee table, one of her colorful pillows under the heel serving as a cushion. In sleep he appeared less intimidating than he had while barking out orders. But even in slumber he wore a grimace that pulled at the corners of his mouth. Add a wheelchair and a cane, and it should have made him vulnerable. Only none of that did.

Nor did it take away from his overall good looks. With his chiseled cheekbones and square jaw, the man was handsome. No getting around that, even in his diminished physical state. Nor was there any getting around his reputation as a playboy. His polished looks and extensive bank account made him quite a catch.

Sierra tiptoed past him, eager to avoid further unpleasantness. At the door, she chanced a glance back. The less interaction she had with her boss, the better.

Phoenix woke to the sound of the door closing. He straightened on the sofa and turned his neck to one side and then the other. Yet another sore muscle for Adam to work on during their evening session. If Phoenix went. Perhaps he'd skip it again. It was this kind of thinking that made him angry, as it also left him feeling defeated. He wanted to get better, but what if he never did? What if the physicians were right?

Phoenix rose unsteadily to his feet, bearing as much of his weight as possible on the cane. He hated it. He hated that it shouted to the world that Phoenix Chamberlain was no longer the man he used to be.

But he had been right to come to Seaside Haven. He'd come here to find a purpose. Something, anything, to give his life meaning if it turned out that all of the physicians were right about his prognosis.

The best memories of his childhood were rooted here. The place had been his sanctuary, both during his grandfather's illness and after his death. Where his relationship with his parents had always been rocky, a young Phoenix had been the apple of his grandfather's eye.

He wondered what his grandfather would think if he could see Phoenix now. His bum leg wouldn't be an issue. But what had he done with his life. His grandfather had put his trust in Phoenix. He had left him his fortune and all of his real estate, not the least of which was the resort.

"Everything that I have will be yours someday." Phoenix could hear his grandfather's raspy voice as he'd made the promise. "I know you'll take good care of the resort, because you love it here as much as I do."

Guilt settled over Phoenix now like a thick blanket of fog. Yeah, he'd loved it so much he hadn't been back since his grandfather passed away. Thank God Sierra was so good at her job. She'd restored the aging resort and had brought in record profits as well. When all was said and done, Phoenix would see to it that she was properly compensated.

"Do you need anything, Mr. Chamberlain?" The question came from Adam, who with Tommy's help, was bringing in the weight bench Phoenix thought of as a torture device.

"I'm going to lie down for a little while," he replied bitterly.

Adam frowned at his reply. "Do you think that's a good idea, sir? Your muscles are probably stiff from the drive over, especially since we didn't get in a session this morning."

Adam was being diplomatic. His choice of wording made it sound as if the omission of the morning session had been an oversight rather than because Phoenix had refused to get out of bed.

"I'm going to lie down," Phoenix repeated, heading in the direction of the bed.

Adam shrugged his shoulders as if to say suit yourself.

Tommy cleared his throat. "As soon as we finish, I'm going to take off if that's okay with you sir?"

Tommy Wynn had worked for the Chamberlain's for a decade; more often Phoenix's designated driver than not. Sometimes he also stepped in the role of bouncer when party guests got out of control. There hadn't been much need for the latter the past few months since Phoenix's partying days were over.

"This mishap of yours might be for the best," his mother had said just that morning. "You have to grow up sometime Phoenix. You need to make sound investments for your future. God knows your father didn't learn that before it was too late."

"I'd say you made out well," he'd responded.

She'd pursed her lips at his sarcastic remark, causing fine lines to feather around her mouth. At fifty-five, Betty

Chamberlain Faulk remained a beautiful woman thanks to the skills of an expensive plastic surgeon.

"I did what was necessary." All these years later, her second husband remained a source of friction between her and Phoenix.

He tried to block out the words his mother had said.

"Mr. Chamberlain?"

Phoenix glanced over his shoulder, realizing he'd never answered Tommy.

"Fine," he replied.

Tommy offered a jaunty salute. He always seemed to be in a good mood. Same for Adam. Phoenix used to be like that, too. He missed his old disposition as much as he missed his mobility.

"I assume Miss Ramstad cleared out her belongings."

Adam answered this time. "Yes sir, Sierra moved her things to the other room and I got all of your things put away."

Phoenix barely heard the last part of his reply. First name basis. For a reason he couldn't fathom, he didn't' like Adam's familiarity with her.

"The last time I saw her, she was on the phone in her office." Adam added before he and Tommy turned to walk away.

Draped in the frumpy red vinyl raincoat Sierra had fit his preconceived notion perfectly. But once she peeled it off and shoved the damp blond hair from her face, she wasn't at all what he'd expected. Phoenix found her attractive, which was a surprise in itself. She wasn't anything like the flashy women, whose beauty relied on a lot of enhancement including breast augmentation that usually caught his attention. Sierra was pretty in an understated way. What would she look like dressed up for a night on the town? He silently answered himself with a second question. *What did it matter?*

He looked around the room that had been his grandfather's. The bedding had been turned down; the lines that peeked from beneath the comforter were creased in places, leaving little doubt that someone had just changed the linens for him. He ran his fingers over the pillowcase. He would be sleeping in her bed. And she would be in the room next to his. He swallowed hard and told himself the sudden upswing in his pulse rate was only because he had a lot to learn from the efficient Miss Ramstad if he hoped to operate the resort as capably as she had been.

Phoenix was done shirking all responsibility. Life as he'd known it was over in more ways than one. In the meantime, he had an appointment with an orthopedic surgeon the following week. He hoped to receive a better prognosis than the one the previous physicians had given him.

As if on cue, his leg muscles began to cramp and spasm. He leaned on the door frame to the bathroom to take the weight off of his left leg. When he glanced up, he spotted the words *Non-habit forming* written in red lipstick on the mirror, accompanied by a bottle of over-the-counter pain pills on the counter.

He studied his reflection in the mirror. The dark circles under his eyes and gaunt cheeks no longer took him by surprise. But it came as a jolt to realize he was smiling.

Chapter Three

A couple of hours later, Sierra was in the resort's galley-style kitchen helping the chef with dinner preparations when the swinging doors opened up and her unwanted guest lumbered inside.

Chef Bijon Invar looked up from the pot of soup he was stirring on the stovetop.

"Sorry, but guests aren't allowed in the kitchen," the chef said politely, but firmly in his thick accent.

The kitchen was Bijon's domain, and he didn't care for guests breaching its doors. To call him temperamental would be putting it mildly. But he was a good chef, with over twenty years of experience operating some of the finest restaurants in New York. Sierra considered it a major coup that she'd managed to hire Bijon on as the head chef.

Phoenix's brow raised in surprise. It was a good bet that he wasn't used to being told where he could and could not go, especially on property that he owned.

Hoping to ward off a battle of the egos, Sierra chimed in, "I think we can make an exception for this guest since he signs our paychecks."

"Mister Chamberlain?" the chef quizzed, his tone brimming with disbelief. His gaze shifted to his cane. "I didn't recognize you..."

Bijon was known for his innovative dishes but not so much for his tact. Sierra decided she would make the introduction.

"Mr. Chamberlain, this is Bijon Invar, the resort's chef. You're in for a treat at dinner. He is making his specialty, pan-seared grouper in an herbed butter sauce."

"Sounds delicious." He acknowledged the chef with a perfunctory nod, but his gaze strayed to Sierra and his eyes narrowed. "And why are *you* wearing an apron?"

"I'm just lending a hand with prep. Nothing that requires a culinary degree."

Eyes still narrowed, Phoenix asked, "Do you help out often, Miss Ramstad?"

His questioned seemed rooted in curiosity, rather than genuine concern.

"I wouldn't say often, but I do what is needed, whether that's here in the kitchen or someplace else at the resort."

Indeed, during her tenure as manager, Sierra had changed soiled linens and a dozen other less-than-glamourous jobs. She figured her willingness to roll up her sleeves was why she had earned the staff's respect.

Phoenix rubbed his chin. "I see."

Unfortunately, Sierra couldn't tell from his expression whether he thought this was a good use of her managerial skills or not. Squaring her shoulders, she asked, "Was there something you needed, Mr. Chamberlain?"

"No. Just taking a look around as so much has changed." From his tone, she couldn't tell if he was happy about that or feeling nostalgic for the past.

Speaking of changes, Phoenix had undergone a bit of transformation as well. His black hair was wet as if he'd recently showered. He wore it combed back from his forehead but a few curls fell across his brow. His face was shaved, all shadow gone from his angular jawline. But it wasn't the absence of the stubble that caught her attention. It was the absence of a grimace.

"I see you took me up on my offer."

The faintest smile lurked on his lips when he asked, "How do you know?"

"Well, you look…rested."

Despite his obvious weight loss, the man was definitely handsome. He had on a crisp white shirt that was tucked into a pair of khaki dress pants. The carved wooden cane in his hand added to his air of sophistication.

"I got in a nap," he announced.

"And a therapy session?" Sierra quizzed.

"No, I was trying to relieve some of the pain. Don't let Adam's baby face fool you. He can be brutal."

Phoenix's subtle attempt at humor came as a nice surprise. She decided to return it.

"They say no pain, no gain."

Just that quickly, his expression changed. She gave an inaudible sigh. Apparently she had reminded him of his slow recovery. While he looked away, Sierra and Bijon traded covert shrugs. Breaking the silence, Phoenix asked, "New ovens?"

"Yes. Last summer."

He glanced around, nodding in approval.

Since it was much easier to talk about business than to exchange pleasantries, Sierra continued. "The walk-in freezer just needed some repairs and it was good as new."

"Excellent." Phoenix nodded, but she got the impression he wasn't listening to what she said.

"Are you hungry? Dinner won't be served for another hour, but…"

He interrupted her. "That's alright. Adam made me an omelet." He sent her a smile that bordered on sheepish. "And he was disappointed that your bread wasn't whole wheat."

"Oh?" Sierra wasn't sure how she felt about guests rummaging through the cupboards. She smiled thinly. "Bijon and I will be going out tomorrow for groceries and supplies for the resort. If you give me a list, I'll be happy to pick up whatever you need."

"I'll have Adam put something together." Phoenix's lip curled. "He likes for me to eat healthy."

"The body is a temple," she chimed.

He snorted. "Mine feels more like an ancient ruin."

Phoenix looked to the far side of the room and his scowl returned to his face. Sierra followed the line of his vision to Bijon's calendar with the days that had passed marked off with red Xs.

"Is something wrong?" she asked.

He shook his head, and without another word, turned and limped out of the kitchen.

"Real friendly, isn't he," Bijon muttered sarcastically.

Sierra picked up her knife and returned her attention to the vegetables on the cutting board. "He'll be gone before we know it and things will be back to normal." At least she hoped that would be the case.

Seeing the days marked off the calendar and realizing that three months had passed since the accident spoiled Phoenix's mood. The ibuprofen Sierra had given him had taken the edge off his physical pain. His emotional pain, however, was another matter.

Phoenix wished the storm would subside so that he could sit on the deck and watch the waves rise and fall. The ocean had always had a calming effect on his emotions. Even on days such as this one, the waves crashed ruthlessly against the shore, but the water always receded and eventually calmed. Soon enough, the sun would come out and chase away the gloom, and the beach would be the same as it had been before the storm. Nothing about his life was predictable, except for his bad leg and the pain that came with it.

Phoenix realized how much he missed his grandfather. Phoenix Chamberlain, Sr., had been the only loving adult in the young Phoenix's life. After his father's death, his mother had remarried, and Phoenix had been shunted aside. Even now Phoenix refused to consider how desperate his mother must have felt to find her financial stability stripped from her. During his last visit to the resort, as they'd sat in this very room, his grandfather had told him, "I don't condone the way your mother has treated you since remarrying, but try to see things from her perspective."

"What do you mean?" he'd asked.

His grandfather had laid his wrinkled hand on Phoenix's shoulder.

"I loved your dad dearly, but I'm not blind to his shortcomings. He made some poor choices over the years. Choices that your mother has had to deal with."

"What are you saying?"

"I'm saying, make me proud, Phoenix."

A final request that Phoenix had failed to honor.

"Mr. Chamberlain?" Adam poked his head around the door.

Although Phoenix was awake, he kept his eyes closed and feigned sleep. He'd been lying on the bed in his room reminiscing and trying to work out the details of his plan. A plan that Sierra wasn't going to like when he eventually told her about it.

His grandfather had left Phoenix the resort with the expectations he would actually run it, rather than sign checks and authorize purchases when he took a break from the ski slopes.

"Mr. Chamberlain?" Adam called again.

Leave me alone! Phoenix shouted the words to himself but didn't say them out loud. He was tired of being sullen and contrary, even as he felt powerless to change his mood. So he kept his eyes closed and his breathing deep and even. He expected that Adam would go away and Phoenix would continue to sulk in silence.

But his physical therapist wasn't alone.

"He's sleeping soundly," Phoenix heard Adam whisper to whoever was with him. "Just go in and get what you need."

"I'd hate to disturb him." Sierra replied.

Once again Phoenix found himself wanting to shout, *leave me alone!* His reason this time was embarrassment. When he'd returned to his room, he'd shucked off his other clothes and now lay atop the comforter wearing a pair of navy nylon shorts. He was shirtless and his pale frame was an imitation of the tanned, physically fit man he'd been. Still, it would be the lesser of two evils, if Sierra's gaze remained on his chest and didn't deviate to the web of scars on his leg.

"Perhaps I should come back later," she said.

"You'd rather see him when he's awake?" Adam's tone was wry and teasing.

Sierra laughed and Phoenix bristled inwardly. Her laughter with the younger man grated his nerves.

"That's a good point," she said.

Footsteps sounded then. Was Adam leaving? Where was Sierra? Phoenix listened for the creak of the floor or the rustle of fabric, anything to announce that she was inside the room. Finally, he heard a door squeak. He chanced opening his eyes. Sierra was in the walk-in closet, standing under the light. He studied her figure as she rose up on her toes, stretching to fetch something from one of the shelves. After she had whatever it was that she'd come in to get, Phoenix watched her turn off the light and gently close the closet door.

She tiptoed toward the bedroom door, but then stopped at the foot of the bed. If she would have looked at his face, she would have realized he was awake. But she wasn't looking at his face. She was studying his leg. The calf was noticeably smaller that its counterpart on his right leg. Adam attributed the disparity to muscle atrophy, although he couldn't guarantee Phoenix that regular exercise would fix that.

Her gaze wandered up to his knee before skimming his thigh. She gaped at the jagged scars where bone had ripped through his flesh and multiple surgeries had followed. She closed her eyes briefly. Did he disgust her?

Did she pity him? He wasn't sure which reaction would be worse. He only knew he couldn't tolerate anymore of her examination.

"Have you seen enough?"

Sierra nearly dropped the scarf she'd retrieved from the closet.

"You scared me!"

Looking for a confrontation, he propped up on one elbow. "You didn't answer my question, Miss Ramstad."

"I didn't mean to stare. I was just…"

She cleared her throat. Even in the dim light, he could see that she was flustered and probably embarrassed. But definitely not aroused. Why would she be? He was repulsive. Angrily he spat out in a suggestive tone, "My leg might not be in working order, but I assure you that everything else is."

She dropped the scarf, and her hand flew to her face. "Excuse me?"

"You heard me."

At that, he expected her to stomp out of the room in a huff. He should've known his smart and sassy resort manager would do no such thing. Instead, Sierra drew closer to his side of the bed.

"I heard you. I was trying to give you the benefit of the doubt."

"And you expect me to apologize?" he said, keeping his tone brazen.

"Well, as a matter of fact I do." She fisted her hands but let them rest on her hips and sent him a convex stare.

Given Phoenix's position on the bed, he admired her rounded hips and firm backside causing parts of his body that had been dormant for too long to awaken. Some of the frustration and anger dissipated, only to be replaced by feelings that were far more dangerous. Even though Phoenix knew he was playing with fire he couldn't keep his eyes from traveling up Sierra's slender frame and lingering on all of the parts that interested him.

"Well?" she demanded.

Their eyes met. Collided was more like it. Phoenix didn't see sparks fly but he felt them as they showered his bare skin. The sensation was one he had never felt and he reveled in it. Afraid he may never feel this way again.

"You first," he taunted.

"You expect *me* to apologize to you?" Her tone hovered between incredulous and infuriated. Perversely, he found it sexy. As he did her narrowed eyes and pursed lips.

"That's right."

"What am I to apologize for?" she quizzed.

"Well, you're in my room…uninvited. *A matter that could be remedied easily enough,* his libido whispered before he could quiet it.

"This is…well, *was* my bedroom."

"Technically, as the resort's owner…"

She stopped him there and talked over his clarification of the room's ownership.

"I just came in to get a scarf from the closet. I would have asked permission, her lips twisted on the word, but you were sleeping and I didn't want to disturb you. If you want an apology for that, then, I'm sorry for the inconvenience, Mr. Chamberlain."

She didn't sound sorry. She sounded agitated and ready to combust. Phoenix knew he should stop provoking her, but he couldn't help himself.

"You got your scarf, yet here you are, Sierra! Under the circumstances I think we should be on a first-name basis. Agree?"

"I...I…" she stuttered, glaring at him.

"You were staring at me. Or maybe I should say gawking. The way one does a train wreck."

"I wasn't staring," she insisted.

Phoenix pushed himself up to a sitting position. In doing so, excruciating pain radiated from his knee, shooting down to his ankle. He wasn't able to bite back his yelp. Apparently, the ibuprofen had worn off.

"Mr. Chamberlain?" she started forward.

"Phoenix, call me Phoenix!" he spat in anger. In that instant, he was back to being angry with himself and everyone else. "Just go."

She turned on her heel and walked out of the room with her shoulders squared and her chin up.

Phoenix flopped back on the bed. His anger dissipated and shame settled in its place. He wondered what it said about him that the most alive he'd felt in months had been while provoking an employee. Sierra was right. He was the one who owed her an apology.

Sierra was enraged. She stomped out of the resort without saying a word to anyone. *Phoenix Chamberlain.* Who did he think he was? She didn't care if he owned Seaside Haven. The man was acting like an inconsiderate tyrant. One with a faulty memory to boot.

He'd agreed with her plan to turn the manager's apartment into a luxurious suite for high-end guests. He'd agreed to let her stay in the unused owner's suite. She had saved their written correspondence to that effect. Maybe she should remind him. Maybe she should return to his room and confront him.

She swallowed, recalling the sight of the man lying on her bed. Maybe she had stared for a couple of minutes longer than was polite. But Phoenix Chamberlain sans shirt and wearing shorts had certainly caught her attention. And since she thought he was asleep, she'd figured she would get a closer look.

She'd gotten an eyeful, all right. The accident had taken a toll on his once-fit body and he was thinner than he'd appeared when fully dressed. Regardless, he was all male, and seeing him spread out on her bed had an unsettling effect on her thinking. And on her breathing.

Sierra tried to recall how long it had been since a man had stirred the air in her lungs. Or that sensation of butterflies in her stomach. She couldn't. Within the first year of her marriage with Turner, things had gone from acceptable to bad. From there, they'd made the leap to awful. In all, three years of her life wasted. It still shamed her to think that she'd allowed herself to be abused for that length of time.

In the immediate aftermath of her ugly divorce, she'd been too shell-shocked to think of dating again. Once she'd moved to Seaside and landed the job at the resort, she'd been happy to focus on her career. It wasn't that she didn't have time for dating. She didn't make time. While staring at Phoenix, Sierra had begun to have second thoughts.

It was after midnight when she finally returned to the resort. Standing in the kitchen now, she rubbed her temples. Adam had the blender on high, making it easy for her to wave and go. But he eyed her knowingly. "What's got you so upset?"

"Not what. Who!"

"I think I can guess who you mean," Adam said, pulling Sierra from her introspection.

Be that as it may, Sierra didn't gossip, much less talk disrespectfully about her boss, so she worked up what she hoped passed for a smile. "I'm just frustrated with one of our suppliers," she said. "He keeps jacking up the prices."

"Supplier, hmm?" Adam didn't look fooled.

Sierra cleared her throat. "I'll just get out of your way. Goodnight."

Chapter Four

Phoenix slept poorly, tossing and turning for the better part of the night. His conscience bothered him as much as his leg. He'd heard Sierra come in, her steps light as she entered the adjacent room. He'd imagined her curled up on the uncomfortable futon, and his conscience nipped at him again. Not because he'd displaced her from her bed, but because his imagination had lingered on what she'd been wearing.

He tossed the covers back. He needed to apologize to her. He'd leave out the part about his wayward imagination and concentrate on his rude behavior from the day before.

He found Sierra on the private deck of the resort. She was seated in one of the lounge chairs, her bible in her lap. A cup of coffee was on a small table next to her. Adam was at the rail drinking a green concoction through a straw. He spotted Phoenix through the sliding glass door and rushed over to open it.

"Good morning, Mr. Chamberlain!" he exclaimed with his usual good cheer. "You're up early. Sierra and I were just enjoying the sunrise."

The man's enthusiasm should have been contagious. Phoenix glanced at Sierra, who looked as unmotivated as he felt.

"Can I get you a smoothie?"

What Phoenix wanted was a cup of high-octane coffee and a couple extra-strength ibuprofen. But what he needed was a few minutes alone with Sierra, and Adam had just provided him the perfect excuse.

"Yes, Adam. A smoothie would be great. Thanks."

Phoenix's response not only had Adam's eyes widening; Sierra stopped reading and turned to look at him.

"You're always pushing about their health benefits," Phoenix added.

"I didn't think you were listening," the younger man replied with comical honesty.

"I'll also take a cup of coffee and a couple ibuprofen when you get a chance."

Adam grinned. "Coming right up. Do you need anything, Sierra?"

She shook her head. "No thanks."

Once they were alone, Phoenix moved to the lounge chair next to hers. Bearing his weight on the cane, he tried to lower himself slowly, but his knee gave out halfway down and he landed on the seat with a plop. He grunted and surprised them both by admitting, "It's so depressing to need assistance taking a seat."

She studied him for a moment before nodding in agreement. Then she went back to her bible.

He tried again. "It's a nice morning. The calm after the storm."

She nodded again, this time without looking up. It was not even six am and Sierra was showered, dressed and on the deck. Most of the women he knew would have been asleep after a late night of partying.

Phoenix cleared his throat, but the words still stuck before finally coming out. "I…I owe you an apology for how I acted yesterday."

"Yes. You do." Her tone was straightforward.

Phoenix rubbed a hand over the stubble on his jaw. "Could you maybe stop reading for a minute and look at me?"

She read a few more words, exhaled slowly and then closed the book. Turning in her seat, she gave him her full attention. He almost wished she hadn't. Big green eyes fringed with amazingly long lashes left him feeling vulnerable.

"I am sorry…the things I said…I was out of line."

"Apology accepted." She lifted her hand and ran her fingers through her hair in a gesture that struck him as almost tentative. "I should have waited to get my scarf."

"You left it on the floor, by the way."

"I know."

He reached into the pocket of his robe and pulled out the crumpled piece of fabric. "Here you go."

A smile tugged at her lips. "Thanks."

"We got off on the wrong foot." He snorted at his unintentionally apropos phrasing. Since humbling himself wasn't as difficult as he'd presumed it to be, he continued, "I should have realized that my early arrival here would cause some chaos."

"Can I ask you something?" she said after a moment.

"Sure."

"Did you even read the monthly reports?" Her tone held a note of censure. The woman certainly didn't pull any punches.

"No. I glanced at them." He decided he owed her the truth. "Well, some of them."

His stomach took a surprising roll. It had been a long time since Phoenix had cared what someone thought of him. Not since his grandfather.

"I should have read them." A responsible owner would have, he admitted to himself. "But I did and still do trust you and your judgment. Besides, we graduated from the same college."

"*You* have a degree?"

The shock on her face was unmistakable and reflected in the disbelief in her tone. Phoenix's battered ego took yet another blow.

"I haven't put it to use, but yes, I have a degree, earned a few years before you would have started classes.

When I interviewed you for the job – which he'd done by phone between runs down the Swiss Alps – I was impressed by your credentials, even though you didn't have much experience."

Her expression turned oddly guarded and she looked away.

"I got married right after graduation." She paused. "My husband didn't think I needed to work."

"You're married?" That came as a surprise. An unpleasant one based on the way his stomach churned. Phoenix rallied as quickly as he could, hoping that none of his dismay showed in his expression. Her marital status was none of his business, legally or otherwise.

"Happily divorced," she replied. Her jaw clenched after she said it and she reached for her cup of coffee.

He couldn't help but be intrigued. Not only about what had happened to end Sierra's marriage, but what kind of man would have let her go. But he kept his questions to himself. Business was the basis of their relationship. And when it came to business, in spite of the degree he'd earned, Phoenix had a lot to learn.

Sierra was no longer clenching her jaw. In fact, he heard excitement in her voice and saw a spark in her eyes as she told him, "I saw so much potential for change the first time I toured the resort. The oceanfront view is amazing." She motioned to the horizon where the sun blazed gold and orange before blurring into shades of pink.

"The resort should have been booked year-round. Yet it had vacancies during the peak tourist seasons. And the internet reviews were dismal. People want amenities when they go on vacation. Give them what they want and they'll come back again."

"I may not have read every one of your reports, but that much I figured out."

"I would imagine the bottom line speaks for itself," she said dryly.

He nodded. "It speaks volumes." Revenues were up and the money he'd invested in upgrades would be repaid in no time. His future was secure, financially at least.

And he owed it all to Sierra.

Guilt throbbed like a bad tooth since his new plan would see her displaced from her job. But he doubted someone of Sierra's caliber would want to stay on, basically sharing managerial duties with him. He'd offer her the option, of course. As much as he wanted to run the resort, he didn't plan to work seven days a week like she apparently did.

If she left, more likely when, he would see to it that she was nicely compensated. He made a mental note to meet with his attorney to draft up a generous severance package when he went into Atlanta for his doctor appointment.

"Thank you," he told her now.

Then he reached over and laid one of his hands over hers. The gesture was intended to be companionable, but the way his body responded to the benign contact was far immoral in nature.

She pulled her hand away, using it to tuck a few strands of hair behind her ear. Her cheeks had turned a becoming shade of pink, and he couldn't help wondering if it was the contact that had thrown her or his gratitude.

Finally, she replied, "The year-end bonus I received was thanks enough." She picked up her coffee cup then and focused her attention on its contents. "I like living here at the resort. And I love my job. I'm good at what I do."

He found the last comment odd. She seemed to be trying to convince him of her competence. If so, she needn't have bothered.

While he covertly studied Sierra's profile, she sipped her coffee and gazed at the horizon. He took in the slope of her nose and her delicate jaw that ended in a perfectly rounded chin. Her beauty stirred him in a way he found both compelling and concerning. The squawk of seagulls and slap of waves on the sand were the only sounds to break the silence until the door opened and Adam stepped out onto the deck. He carried a tray that held a cup of coffee and a glass filled with a green concoction.

"Here you go, Mr. C. One smoothie as requested. I took the liberty of adding a banana." The young man grinned. "They're an excellent source of potassium."

"Yum." Phoenix grimaced. He hated bananas as much as he hated smoothies.

"Well, I need to meet Bijon to go shopping. I have your list," Sierra told Adam. Then she rose to her feet, book in her hand, her gaze fixed on Phoenix. "Enjoy your smoothie."

Was it his imagination or was she biting back a smile?

Chapter Five

Since his arrival at Seaside Haven, Phoenix had been up each day by dawn. He'd felt more rested the past few days than he had during the past several years. This morning he couldn't claim to feel the same. Phoenix had slept sporadically when he'd slept at all. That was because his appointment with the doctor was today. He didn't want to believe that nothing more could be done when it came to his recovery but it was a good possibility that this physician would tell him the same thing all of the other physicians had. The same stifling sense of defeat that had defined his life for the past three months settled over him.

After lying in bed, his mind racing as much as it was wandering, he finally threw back the covers and struggled out of bed. His leg was stiff. It always was first thing in the morning. He performed a couple of the stretching exercises Adam recommended and then got dressed in his usual attire of khaki pants and a light-weight-shirt.

As he passed the adjacent room, he noticed that the door was ajar. He glanced inside, doubting as he did so that he would find Sierra there.

At this hour, she would be out on the deck, a cup of coffee on the table at her side and the bible on her lap. It was how she started her days unless the weather was bad. So, for the past week, coffee on the deck was how Phoenix had started his days as well.

Movement inside of the room caught his attention. Not only was Sierra there, she was undressing. He should look away. But he couldn't. He stood rooted in place, gaze fixated on her slim body. Her movements were practical, hardly choreographed to seduce. Still, the sight of her smooth skin and lean contours made it difficult to breathe.

He managed to inhale, and a familiar and all too pleasing aroma filled his nostrils. Clean and crisp with a hint of floral. It was the same fragrance that teased him at night while he lay in her bed. The sheets may have been fresh, but her scent was all around the room. Making him yearn. The heat enveloped him now. He took a couple of steps backward and cleared his throat noisily in an effort to announce his presence. When he drew even with the door a second time, Sierra was pulling it open.

"Good morning, Phoenix," she said.

"Good morning."

She'd exchanged the blue shirt she usually wore for a lighter version with the resort's logo embroidered on the chest and he found himself staring at her breasts. He ripped his gaze away only to have it settle on the tangled sheets that littered the futon bed behind her. He frowned.

"That doesn't look very comfortable," he murmured.

Sierra glanced over her shoulder. "Probably not as comfortable as the pillow top mattress you're sleeping on," she agreed. "But it's not bad."

He grimaced. "I'm sorry for the inconvenience my stay has caused you."

Her eyes widened fractionally, but that was the only indication his words surprised her. She nodded. "It's okay."

He changed the subject. "I thought you'd be out on the deck."

"I was, but I spilled coffee on my shirt."

"So, that's why you changed it." He realized his faux pas even before her eyes narrowed.

"How long have you been up?" she asked.

"Up?" he shrugged, surprised by her question.

"You know, awake? You have a doctor's appointment today, right?"

Her gazed lowered to the cane gripped in his hand. "Right." *And an appointment with his attorney,* Phoenix added silently.

"I'll say a prayer for you."

"Thanks." He frowned at the cane. "I'm hoping for a more promising prognosis."

"And if you don't get it? What then?"

Phoenix took a deep breath and exhaled slowly. "To be honest with you, I don't know what I'll do. At what point do I just...give up." His fingers tightened on the cane's handle until his knuckles turned white.

"You can't expect to fully recover if you don't put in the effort."

He made a scoffing noise. No one had dared say such a thing to him. Even Adam trod lightly when it came to admonishing Phoenix for his lack of effort.

Instead of telling her to go to hell, he replied with similar honesty. "Some days everything seems so...pointless."

The admission hung between them, suspended in the ensuing silence. Something flickered in her eyes. Was it understanding? Empathy?

"That is depression doing the talking," she said after a moment. Her tone was filled with compassion, which only made it worse.

Since he was already feeling helpless, his pride made him retort, "What are you a psychiatrist now?"

She appeared to take his irritable tone in stride. "No. I just know that when a person is at his or her lowest point, it's not always easy to get back up."

"Sounds as if you're speaking from experience?"

She eyed him for a moment before speaking again.

"I'm heading back out to the deck. I have a few more emails to reply to before I get to work. Are you coming?"

Her switch in topics made it clear she knew something about how difficult it was to climb one's way back up after hitting the bottom. Her divorce seemed the obvious culprit so he let the matter drop.

"Can I get you a cup of coffee? I'll even carry it for you," she offered with a smile that seemed more flirtatious than merely friendly. He decided to think of that as progress.

Phoenix followed her. His pace was slow and measured compared to her brisk one, and far less graceful. The view was well worth it, he thought, as his gaze dipped south to watch her hips swing side to side. His interest was piqued again.

"Is Adam out on the deck already?" he asked.

"No. He went for a run on the beach but he should be back within the hour. I'm sure he'll be happy to make you one of those smoothies then."

Phoenix groaned.

She stopped at the granite topped island in the kitchen and poured coffee before starting for the door that led to the deck.

It was breezier this morning than it had been on previous days. The wind caught her hair and pushed several strands of it across her face. She finger-combed them back after sitting their coffee on a table and settling onto her lounge chair. His fingers itched to touch her hair. To touch her.

By the time Phoenix had his legs stretched out in front of him, Sierra was already tapping on the computer's keyboard. While he appreciated her above-and-beyond the call of duty approach, it wasn't expected. Nor was it particularly healthy. He nearly chuckled aloud at that thought. As if he had any right to judge another person's lifestyle.

He glanced idly at the computer screen, expecting to see her replying to business-related emails or confirming reservations.

"Do you always read other people's correspondence?" she inquired blandly.

"No…sorry. I assumed that whatever you were writing was business-related."

"I do have a life, you know," she said as if trying to convince him.

Not much of one he thought but kept his opinion to himself. He did ask, "Who is Ryan?"

Her former husband? Her lover?

She gave him her full attention, cat-green eyes blazing with an emotion he couldn't pinpoint. "She is my niece," she answered.

"Lucky you." When she frowned, he added, "I am an only child. No siblings, no nieces or nephews. Just me."

With his father and grandfather deceased and his mother estranged, that was the case.

"I have a twin sister, Sienna." Her expression softened, and a smile lurked around the corners of her mouth.

"Are you two close?"

"Yes." Now she frowned again. "Well, not as close as I'd like. My brother-in-law, Del, was a police officer…he was killed in the line of duty. It's taken a toll on my sister."

"God, I'm sorry, Sierra," Phoenix said, although the words seemed inadequate under the circumstances. In some ways it made his own struggles seem minor, especially since his accident had been the result of aggressive paparazzi side-swiping the car he was riding in rather than something as honorable as protecting and serving others. It was a humbling realization.

"Ryan is five now. For the past couple of summers, she and my sister have come to Seaside over the Fourth of July holiday."

"So they'll be coming this summer?" he asked, oddly envious of the picture of domestic bliss that her words had conjured up.

"They stay with me, Phoenix. And there's no room at the resort," she replied.

It took him a moment to realize what she meant. He was staying in *her* room.

"Don't worry about it. What's done is done. I promised Ryan that she and her mom can come another time, maybe during Christmas."

The assumption being that Phoenix wouldn't be at Seaside Haven then. He swallowed. He wasn't planning on going anywhere.

While she went back to typing, he skimmed their surroundings. White-capped waves danced on the horizon before crashing to shore. Down the beach, he spotted Adam. He was a physically fit young man and Phoenix envied him.

"Are you a runner?" he asked Sierra, as he pointed in the direction of his physical therapist.

"No," she replied. "Running is hard on the knees. That's why I walk on the beach. Besides, I am a seashell addict."

He recalled the assortment of glass containers of various shapes and sizes nestled around the lobby and in her bedroom and bath. Some people paid an interior decorator to bring in such touches, but Sierra had collected them herself.

"Do they have a twelve-step program for seashell addicts?"

She laughed. "I can't believe you actually made a joke."

He blinked. "I used to have a good sense of humor."

"Did you break that in the car accident, too?"

He laughed aloud, a raspy sound that scraped his throat as it came out.

"You're funny!"

Sierra closed her computer and rose to her feet just as Adam jogged up the steps that led from the beach. "Enjoy your run?" she asked as she sent Phoenix a wink.

"Y-yeah! Great…morning…for it," Adam replied, breathing heavily. "Hope you get a good report at your doctor's appointment," he added, having fully caught his breath. "I'm going inside for a shower."

Adam's comment brought back Phoenix's anxiety about seeing the specialist and his attorney in Atlanta. He rubbed his thigh. The daily regimen of ibuprofen had dulled the pain, but nothing was successful in taking it away completely.

"Are you afraid?" Sierra asked.

He shook his head as if to say no, but answered, "A little."

He swung his legs over the side of lounge chair and grabbed the railing, using his upper body strength, he levered to his feet. The breeze picked up, whipping several strands of blonde hair across Sierra's face. This time, Phoenix gave in to impulse and tucked it behind her ear before she could. Afterward, his hand lingered to her check. It was as soft as silk, just as he'd imagined.

He watched her eyes widen in surprise or interest. He needed to believe it was the latter. He needed to believe that *she* found him desirable. He caressed her check and her lips parted ever so slightly, and Phoenix leaned in for a kiss. When she didn't resist, he went back for more.

He settled his mouth firmly over hers this time. She rose on her tiptoe and tilted her head to one side. Without breaking off their kiss, she dropped the laptop onto the lounge chair's cushion. Both of her hands were free now, and she brought them up to his shoulders.

Raw and unrestrained passion coursed through Phoenix's veins. For the first time in months, he felt alive again. He kept one hand on the rail for support. But something told him that even if both of his legs had been in working order, his knees would have felt weak.

Sierra pulled back slowly, blinking up at him as if in disbelief. Although her hands remained on his shoulders, the moment was ending. He traced her lips with the pad of his thumb and felt her quiver.

"Phoenix, I don't think…" Her voice was barely above a whisper. He leaned closer to her and she shook her head. She dropped her arms to her sides and backed up a step. Then, turned and hurried inside, leaving him alone on the deck.

Chapter Six

Phoenix wanted to throw his cane across the doctor's office or plow his fist into the doctor's face, as if it were somehow the man's fault that Phoenix's leg was shattered beyond repair.

"You need to accept that your life has changed," the doctor was saying. "You need to find new hobbies, Mr. Chamberlain." The doctor cleared his throat, then added, "I also recommend therapy."

"I'm in therapy!" Phoenix spat out.

"I'm not talking about physical therapy," the doctor announced, his expression kind and condescending. Phoenix balled his hands into fists in his lap in an attempt to keep from punching a hole in the wall. He stayed that way for the remainder of the appointment.

"I'm sorry, Mr. C," Tommy began as they left the doctor's office. "I know you were hoping for better news."

Phoenix didn't answer. Once they were in the Escalade, he barked an address at Tommy. At least his attorney wouldn't be able to contradict Phoenix's plans for his future. With so much else beyond his control, he needed to be in charge of something and the resort was all he had left.

Sierra had remained at the desk in her office for most of the day. She was still mentally berating herself for kissing Phoenix when she heard footsteps in the hall outside of her office. One set was uneven and accompanied by the distinctive click of a cane on the tile. The other was heavier. Phoenix and Tommy had returned from the doctor appointment.

Sierra exhaled through her mouth, then rose to her feet. On her way to the door, she smoothed her hair and schooled her expression into one of polite concern.

"How did the…?"

That was all she got out before Tommy shook his head.

Meanwhile, Phoenix never even glanced her way. He glared straight ahead with his jaw clenched, his dark eyebrows pinched in a scowl reminiscent of the expression he'd been wearing the first time they met. Whatever the physician had said, it hadn't been good news. Her heart sank. This, she knew, was Phoenix's worst fear.

That evening, Phoenix requested to have dinner in his room. Sierra had prepared the tray herself while Adam was creating some kind of smoothie. "Just leave the tray on the counter and I'll take it when I finish with this," he said as he added slices of banana to the blender. She nodded. The less interaction with Phoenix the better. For both of them.

She raised her voice so that Adam could hear. "So, bad news today?'

Adam stopped the blender and sighed. "Not necessarily bad news. Just not what he wanted to hear. He won't be skiing down the slopes again. And he's probably never going to walk without a limp and a cane. The faster he accepts that and moves on with his life, the better off he's going to be." He resumed the blender, rendering conversation impossible.

Sierra's heart had ached for Phoenix. But she stopped feeling sorry for him when, a week later, he remained in his room with the curtains drawn. Adam had been the only person allowed to enter, and then only to bring his meals.

At first, she'd been relieved that Phoenix hadn't joined her for coffee on the deck in the mornings. After that kiss they'd shared, things between them were bound to be awkward. But now, five days after his doctor appointment, she was out of both empathy and patience.

"You didn't have to take dinner to Phoenix?" she quizzed Adam.

"I am heading to the dining room to eat and I will take dinner to him when I have finished." He glanced at his watch. "It's early for your evening walk. It hasn't cooled off much outside yet."

Indeed, it was still hot, which is why she usually waited until late evening to walk on the beach. It was mostly empty by then, even the hardcore sunbathers having packed up for the day. "I know, but there's no new guests arriving and the dinner crowd was light because of the festival happening in town."

She inclined her head down the hallway. "Has he been out of his room today?"

"No, never even got out of bed." Adam shook his head. "He's going to be extra sore once he decides to rejoin the land of the living and resumes physical therapy."

Sierra pursed her lips and shook her head.

"I know what you're thinking," Adam said.

"That he's not only feeling sorry for himself but also sabotaging his recovery? When Adam didn't reply, Sierra demanded, "Well, am I wrong?"

"Not in the least."

This reply didn't come from Adam. It came from Phoenix, who was standing in the hallway, just outside the door to his room.

She swallowed hard. "I'm sorry."

"Oh, please. Don't ruin your frankness with an apology," he told Sierra as he trudged toward her. "Your honesty is one of the qualities I like about you."

He was looking for a fight, and she wouldn't disappoint him. She lifted her head, squaring her chin. "You're right. I'm not sorry. What I am is disappointed!"

Phoenix's dark brow elevated in surprise at that. "Disappointed?" he repeated.

Adam picked that moment to mumble something about having dinner before he walked away. Phoenix waited until the door closed behind him before he continued. "Well, you can get in line behind my mother! I've never been able to please her either." He shook his head and some of the rage went out of him. "Didn't Adam tell you? This is it Sierra! What you see is what you get!"

The comment momentarily caught Sierra off guard. But she chose not to dwell on his last statement. Instead, she remained focused on the subject at hand; his reaction to the physician's prognosis. Taking a step closer to him, she said, "You're not going to be able to ski the slopes in Europe again, or run a marathon. Even ballroom dancing may be out of the question."

Phoenix's voice thundered through the resort. "I don't need you to remind me of all the things I can no longer do!" The mocking smile he sent her vanished when he lost his balance. He was able to catch himself on the nearby door frame, but in doing so he had let go of the cane. The gold-tipped walking aid clattered to the floor and vicious cursing followed.

Sierra allowed him to vent his frustration, waiting until he was done to retrieve the cane and hold it out to him. He snatched it from her grip. She needed to make Phoenix use his anger to his advantage. Channeled correctly, it could prove to be beneficial. God knew she'd used her own anger as a catalyst for change.

So she went on to say, "Well, let me tell you what you can do. You can continue to be a resentful invalid or you can do something about it." She expected her words to get a rise out of him but to her consternation, the fight went out of

Phoenix. His voice lost its hostile edge and he stated, "But I am a bitter invalid."

"Adam said that you would get stronger if you wouldn't skip therapy for days at a time and put in minimal effort when you do it."

"So, you and Adam are discussing my therapy? I wasn't aware that the two of you had gotten so close. Nor that I was a topic of conversation between the two of you."

Phoenix was trying to get to her, but she wouldn't let him. "You know what your problem is?"

He blew out a breath. "I'm sure you'll tell me."

She smiled and went on. "Your problem is that you expect someone else to fix this for you." Her bluntness could wind up costing her career, but no one else was inclined to stand up to him. The sooner he was back on his feet, literally and figuratively, the sooner he would leave the resort and things would get back to normal.

Sierra ignored the twinge of regret the thought of his leaving caused. Instead, she continued on, intentionally discarding any effort to employ politeness. Phoenix needed to hear the unvarnished truth. "You may not be able to do the things you used to, but you can have a happy, fulfilling future."

He cocked his head to one side, eyebrows lifted. "Are you happy, Sierra?"

The question caught her off guard. The way he said it, the way he looked at her had feelings she'd nearly forgotten bubbling inside of her. She chose to ignore his question and took a breath. "We aren't talking about me. We're talking about you. If you want to spend the rest of your life being angry and defeated, then I hope that you'll find somewhere else to do it!"

His mouth flew open in disbelief. "Are you telling me to leave the resort? *My* resort? Because that is what it sounded like to me, Sierra."

"No, that's not what I'm saying. What I am trying to say is that no one wants to be with someone who is angry all of the time."

"You didn't seem all that adverse the other day on the deck." His tone was suggestive as his gaze skimmed down her body before returning to her pouty lips.

"Don't…"

"Don't what?" he challenged her, his tone retaining all of its redolence.

"Don't bring that up." She blinked, in an effort to regroup her thoughts.

Phoenix went on to say, "Seaside Haven is mine. So I'll stay here as long as I please."

"You're right," she agreed calmly, even though her pulse was still racing.

"And I'm sure that you can find another manager."

She loved her job at the resort. She would be distraught to leave here. And to leave Phoenix. She puzzled over her feelings and wondered if she should apologize. She moderated her tone and lowered the volume. "Phoenix, you have a lot to be grateful for. You walked away from a car accident that could've ended your life or left you confined to a wheelchair."

He closed his eyes momentarily, and she thought she may have gotten her point through to him but then he demanded, "Are you finished?"

"I…I guess I am." And Sierra sincerely thought her career was also.

"Good." He turned and pointed to the tray of food that sat untouched. "I'd like to eat on the deck tonight." He started for the door. Apparently, he expected her to carry the tray outside for him.

Sierra picked up the tray. The cheerful yellow flower in the vase mocked her mood. She might be his employee, but she wouldn't be his enabler. "You carry it," she called out after him.

He glared back at her. "I can't and you know it."

"So you know what that means?" She didn't wait for him to respond, but continued. "You need to put more effort in so that you can improve your situation."

"Do you think this is how I want to live?" His voice had turned soft, but she wasn't fooled by the muted tone. He was every bit as angry as he'd been earlier.

"I think…" was as far as she got before he cut her off.

"I hate this!" he shouted, throwing the cane down with such force that it snapped in two. One half flew into the bedroom while the other half flipped end over end before striking Sierra in the face. The jagged piece of wood pierced her flesh. She reached and clapped her hand over the opening.

The color drained from Phoenix's face as he watched in surprise.

"Oh, my God! Sierra, I never meant to do that." He reached for her but she batted his hand away.

More frustrated than anything, she turned and rushed down the hallway, passing a wide-eyed Adam as she sought the refuge of her office.

Chapter Seven

Phoenix was disgusted with himself. Of course he hadn't intended for the cane to snap and strike Sierra, but that was exactly what had happened. His anger had caused her injury and all she'd been trying to do was help him.

He rubbed a hand over his face as he slid down the wall to the floor. Never had he hated himself more. Sierra was right. He had a lot to be grateful for. And his mother had been right. He needed to take responsibility for his life and be the man his grandfather had believed Phoenix could be.

He thought he'd been doing that by coming to Seaside, determined to learn the ropes and eventually take over the day-to-day operations of the resort. But he hadn't come here to heal, he'd come here to hide.

He was still seated on the floor when Adam reached him several minutes later.

"Mr. Chamberlain? Are you all right?" The young man's eyes were wide with concern.

Phoenix wasn't sure how to respond. He wasn't all right, but it had nothing to do with his leg. So, instead of answering Adam's question, he asked, "Can you help me up from here?"

"Sure boss."

With Adam's assistance, Phoenix was soon on his feet.

"What happened to your cane?" Adam asked.

Phoenix's stomach clenched with a mixture of embarrassment and shame. "I'd rather not talk about that."

"Okay, no problem." The therapist bobbed his head in affirmation.

That was Adam, eager to please, but unable to criticize his boss for his lack of effort and bad attitude. Unlike Sierra, who'd called Phoenix on both of them even though it meant she may lose her job. Phoenix pictured her face again and a fresh wave of shame washed over him.

"I'd like to lie down," he announced.

"Right now?" Adam frowned.

"Therapy tomorrow I promise, but right now I have a lot to think about."

The following morning, Adam helped Phoenix out to the deck before the sun was fully up. He'd hoped to find Sierra there, drinking coffee, the bible open on her lap. God knew, he needed to beg for forgiveness. But the deck was empty.

"Looks like we beat Sierra out here today," he said in what he hoped was a conversation starter rather than an attempt to question her whereabouts.

Adam helped lower him into one of the lounge chairs before he replied, "She may be sleeping late today."

"Oh, why is that?" Phoenix asked.

"She didn't get back from the emergency room until after two this morning."

"Emergency room?" Phoenix swallowed hard. "How bad was the gash?"

"Pretty bad but they were able to close it with a few stitches." Adam studied Phoenix without blinking. Questions brewed in his mind but he didn't prod.

Phoenix didn't owe his employee an explanation, but he felt the need to clear the air. "It was my fault. I broke my cane and the halves went flying. One of them struck Sierra in the face." He swallowed again but he couldn't get the bad taste out of his mouth.

Adam glared at his boss. He'd never known the easy-going, carefree man to be violent. "So, it was an accident?" he asked, some of the tension subsiding from his brow.

Phoenix nodded. "Yes, of course, it was an accident. She was only trying to help me."

But it was time that he helped himself. That was the realization Phoenix had come to last night, as he'd replayed his conversation with Sierra and how he'd spent the past three months since the car accident. It had taken a beautiful, blunt-spoken woman to make him see the light.

*****

Sierra changed the bandage on her face. In the two days since her visit to the emergency room, the area surrounding the gash had turned from varicolored red to purple to an unsightly blue. As for the wound itself, it was probably going to leave a scar. But it was her own fault. She'd pushed Phoenix to his breaking point.

For the past few days she'd done her best not only to avoid thinking about him, but to avoid him. She missed her early mornings on the deck, watching the sun disperse golden rays across the horizon. She missed Phoenix. But she took her coffee to her desk and kept the door closed as she worked.

As she replied to the last of the day's emails, a new one dropped into her inbox. She knew the sender well. The subject line read: Need assistance, please

Please? The use of manners was new as was his admitting to needing help. Curiosity got the better of her and she clicked to open the email.

Dear Miss Ramstad, it began. So they were back to courtesy titles. She should have been pleased. But disappointed was what she felt. She shrugged it off and continued reading.

Adam has the night off. Could you bring a dinner tray?

Thank you,

Phoenix

She closed the email and sighed. So much for her efforts to avoid him.

The room was quiet and dark when she entered holding the tray. "Hello?" she called.

"Over here."

His bed. Of course. The last thing she wanted was to confront the lion in his den, but she swallowed and walked over holding the tray aloft. She turned on a lamp at his bedside and set the tray on the nightstand.

Phoenix sat up and rested his back against the upholstered headboard. He wore a t-shirt with a designer logo embroidered on the chest. That was as far as she allowed her gaze to stray.

"Here you go, "she said in lieu of a greeting. "I think you'll enjoy it. Bijon's prime rib gets rave reviews from our guests." With that she turned to leave. She almost made it to the door before Phoenix said, "I think I will have dinner on the deck tonight."

With her back still to him, she grimaced. Then a forced smile curved on her lips as she turned and crossed the room to retrieve the tray. "Sure, Mr. Chamberlain," she said in her most compliant tone.

"I prefer that you call me Phoenix," he told her as he struggled to stand.

"I thought that since your email referred to me as Miss Ramstad…" She let her words trail off and shrugged her shoulders. For the first time since entering the room, she glanced at his face. The dark smudges under his eyes made it look like he'd gone a few rounds in a boxing ring. The growth on his face made it clear he hadn't shaved in days and his hair was unkempt.

His gaze was on the bandage on her face and an emotion she'd never seen before glazed his eyes. Where he had been ill-tempered and bitter at their last meeting, this time he appeared subdued. Her heart warmed in a way that alarmed her.

"Sierra." When he spoke, his voice was hoarse. "Adam told me you had to have stitches. Did the doctor say if it would scar?"

"Probably," she shrugged.

"I'm sorry." He bit off an oath, and reassured her, "I'll pay for you to see a plastic surgeon."

"That won't be necessary. It was an accident."

Angry and bitter, Phoenix had been easier to resist. But standing in front of her humbled and contrite caused her heart to skip a beat and that was before his eyes locked with hers. Under his current gaze she felt more self-conscious than she had when his gaze had first homed in on her bandage.

"Apology accepted," she mumbled before she hurried from the room.

She took his dinner outside, bypassing the lounge chairs and setting the tray on the wrought iron bistro table tucked into the corner of the deck. By the time she returned inside to assist him, he had reached the French doors. She held one side open for him and their bodies brushed as he stepped outside. He stopped and held her gaze.

"Will you stay with me?" Phoenix asked.

"I thought you'd want to be alone."

He took a seat on one of the heavy wrought iron chairs she'd pulled out for him. "I don't know what I want anymore. Except that I'd like for you to stay with me."

Her breath hitched as he stared at her. This was not the same entitled heir who had arrived at the resort mere weeks earlier. Nor was it the bitter man who'd neglected his therapy sessions despite desperately wanting to get stronger.

She slid on to the chair opposite his and adjusted the angle so that she could look out at the ocean. While he ate, she took in the scenery. She'd always loved the view and the privacy of the deck, which was confined on both sides by vine-covered trellises whose blooms scented the sea air.

It was a hot evening, the humidity almost oppressive. Most of the guests preferred the air conditioned dining room to eating alfresco. In truth, she was surprised Phoenix had wanted to come outdoors, but after holing up in his room for a few days, maybe he'd felt the need for fresh air regardless of the heat that accompanied it.

"Hot and humid tonight," he said, as if he could read her mind.

"Yes it is," she replied to make conversation.

Phoenix set his fork aside with a clatter. "You must think I'm the biggest jerk in the world."

Sierra blinked, caught off guard by his statement. "Actually, that title belongs to my ex-husband. Besides, it's not my place to judge you."

"Because I'm your boss?" he quipped.

She could have agreed and left it at that. Perhaps she should have.

"I did a lot of things I'm not proud of when I was…going through a tough time in my life."

"Are you talking about your divorce?"

It wasn't something she talked about often. Even with her sister or mother, Sierra had been stingy with the details. She'd found them too painful to recount, too humiliating to admit to. So she nodded in agreement.

"When it came down to it, I had a choice to make. I could accept things as they were, which was bad, or I could make a change. It sounds easy to do…" she sent him a wry smile, "unless you're the one taking the steps and not sure where you're going to land." She reached across the table and laid her hand over his. "Change is never easy, Phoenix."

He grunted. "I admire you, Sierra."

She blinked in surprise. She wasn't sure what to say.

"Did I render you speechless?" he asked after a long silence.

"More like flattered."

He shifted in his chair and grimaced.

"What did the doctor say about the pain?" she asked.

"It's to be expected." He muttered. "He offered to give me a prescription."

She bobbed her head. "And you turned him down," she guessed.

"Actually, I asked him for a non-narcotic alternative." He picked up his glass and took a sip. His grimace was comical. "I've been meaning to tell you, this tea is dreadful!"

"It's peach tea."

"Sierra, in the South, people drink sweet tea."

"Yes, well, not all of the guests who stay at the resort are from the South. As a matter of fact, they hail from all parts of the states. There should be some sweet tea in the kitchen. I can get you some, if you'd like."

She was already rising when he said, "I'd rather have a glass of wine." When she hesitated, he added, "I'm not driving. Nor am I taking medications that restrict alcohol consumption."

"All right."

As she started for the door, he called out, "Bring two glasses."

"Oh, no wine for me. I'm still on the clock." She winked. "Besides, what would my boss say if he found out I was drinking on the job?"

His gaze had been on the horizon, where the waves were white capping before they churned to shore. Now his eyes shifted to her. "He'd say have someone cover for you."

Suddenly she felt nervous. But she suspected the butterflies in her stomach had a far different origin. "One bottle of red wine and two glasses coming right up."

Chapter Eight

Sierra returned a few minutes later, holding an opened bottle of merlot in one hand and a pair of wine glasses in the other. Her movements were relaxed but sexy. Phoenix sighed, and sent her a genuine smile as he admired her approaching.

She poured the wine, set the bottle aside, and slipped into her seat.

"Thank you," he said.

"For?" Her eyebrows shot up.

"Everything." He sent her a sideways smile as he lifted his glass and tapped it against hers. After the toast, they both took a sip. Then he continued, "This is good, but you should have picked one of the pricier labels from the Rondé Winery."

"This vintage earned a couple of prestigious awards last year, which is why Bijon asked me to order some to serve here at the resort. According to him, it pairs well with the stuffed tenderloin."

Phoenix glanced her way and nodded. "Are you a connoisseur?" he asked.

She took another sip, then replied, "I wouldn't say that."

"I'm sure you know more about wine than I do." He held up his glass as he studied the deep red wine in the waning light. "I've never been able to pick up on the aromas that the experts talk about."

She wrinkled her nose and settled back in her chair.

Phoenix was becoming relaxed. His shoulder muscles, which were always so tense, had started to loosen. And while his leg still ached, he was able to ignore it.

"Don't tell Bijon," she said.

"About the wine?" he quizzed, surprised by her request. "A glass of wine shouldn't hurt you."

Suddenly regretting that she had said anything, she added, "He has this holistic approach to diet and nutrition."

He nodded. "Wine is good for you. In moderation, of course. Besides, Jesus turned water into wine."

Her eyes held as much amusement as challenge when she replied, "Never heard you reference the Holy Bible before."

Phoenix grunted out an affirmation.

She sipped her wine. The sound of the waves and the squawk of seagulls hunting their evening meal occasionally broke the silence. As did snippets of conversation from beachcombers or guests on the resort's public decks.

"I love this place." He didn't realize he had spoken the words aloud until she glanced his way, so he went on. "I came here every summer when I was a child."

"Must have been fun," she murmured.

Phoenix shook his head, reminiscing the days spent here at the resort with his grandfather.

They sat in silence again as the sun began to set. Words weren't necessary with her and he liked that. Most of the women he knew would have become agitated, feeling ignored. Sierra merely sipped her wine, seeming to appreciate the view and the calming sound of the ocean as much as he did.

The resort's shadow crept steadily over the beach as the sun began its descent. Just under half a bottle remained, and Sierra wanted to stay for another round. But before she could say it, he announced, "It's time to call it a night."

"I was thinking the same thing," she said reluctantly, rising to her feet. She touched his shoulder. "This was nice."

Was she referring to the wine? Or spending time with him? But he stopped himself from asking her.

She loaded up the dinner tray while he managed to stand. His muscles were stiff from sitting. He didn't bother trying to camouflage his discomfort. Sierra stepped closer and put one of her arms around his waist for support.

The heat from her fingers radiated through the nylon fabric of his shirt. But what grabbed his libido's attention was the way the side of her breasts pressed against his ribs. Firm but soft at the same time, much like the woman herself. And her attitude appealed to him as much as the curve of her hips or her dark-lashed green eyes.

Phoenix burned with dormant desires. Did she feel it, too? He recalled the kiss they'd shared and his breath hitched.

"Are you okay?' she asked, staring up at him.

"Yeah, I'll be okay," he murmured. "I just need to lie down."

His ardor cooled substantially when he spotted Adam sitting on the sofa in his room. He glanced up from the movie he was watching. "Is everything okay, Mr. C?" he asked as he rose to his feet.

"I thought you and Tommy had gone out for the night." Phoenix said.

"The band wasn't very good so we decided to come back earlier than planned. Let me give you a hand." Adam started forward, but Sierra waved him off.

Phoenix grunted before admitting, "I'm paying the price for my disobedience. You've done your best to help me, Adam. But I haven't been a good patient. That changes tomorrow."

"So, boss, physical therapy at ten?" Adam quizzed, his expression showing pleasure.

"Sure!" Phoenix replied, his gaze shifting to Sierra. "I'm not going to give up!"

Chapter Nine

Sierra slipped from bed before the alarm went off the following morning. She hadn't slept well. Even though she'd dropped off to sleep not too long after her head hit the pillow, she'd awaken just after five. She blamed the wine but she knew it was thoughts of Phoenix that kept her awake.

He could be stubborn but he could also admit when he was wrong. Just when she'd been ready to write him off as shallow, he'd surprised her. The man wasn't as superficial as she'd assumed. Not only was she physically attracted to him, she'd actually begun to like him.

She thought of the glimpses into his life that he had allowed her the previous evening. Apparently, even before the accident, his life was far from perfect. God knew it was easier for her to think of him as pampered and spoiled which to her meant hard to please and hard to love.

Outside her room, Sierra could hear footsteps. She figured it was Adam, eager to start his day. Phoenix's resoluteness the night before had seemed sincere, but would he do his physical therapy today?

"Just a minute," she called when a light tap sounded at the door. She pulled on a robe and loosely tied it for modesty's sake. It wasn't Adam who stood at the doorway, but Phoenix. Some of his hair stuck up at the crown as if he'd just gotten out of bed. Still, her heart somersaulted at the sight of him.

"Morning." His voice was scruffy from sleep but his eyes were alert as he did a quick glance of her body.

Sierra's blood heated.

"Good morning. You're up early."

"I couldn't sleep," he said.

She eyed him for a moment, hoping it had been thoughts of her that had kept him awake. "Are you eager to get started with Adam?"

"Sure." Phoenix tucked his hands into the pockets of his black track pants. But what caught her attention was his University of Georgia t-shirt. She was wearing one just like it.

"Nice shirt," she declared.

He glanced down, then back up at her. "Thanks."

When she pulled the lapels of her robe open to show him her t-shirt, her taut nipples strained against the fabric beneath the UGA logo.

When his gaze lingered, her flesh prickled with desire. Sierra hadn't been with a man since her divorce. For that matter, she'd been on only a few dates, set up by her well-meaning mother.

And when it came to Phoenix she was playing with fire. He owned the resort and he was her boss. Even though this was her home and her career, it was her heart that was at stake. She swallowed and pushed the thought aside. She needed to be smart and level-headed. So she tugged the robes lapels together and folded her arms across her chest.

"Did you need something?" she asked, intending the question to be polite rather than provocative.

Given the desire that burned in his eyes, she had an idea in which direction his mind had veered. God help her she thought to herself as her mind wandered.

He glanced away, then replied, "I wanted to let you know that I won't be having coffee on the deck this morning."

Disappointment washed over her.

When she didn't speak, Phoenix added, "I decided to get the torture session over first thing." A sheepish grin accompanied the words.

"Ah, I see," she quipped, keeping their chat friendly.

At that moment, Adam sauntered down the hallway. He was dressed in a t-shirt and the same style track pants as Phoenix. But unlike his boss, Adam's hair was damp from a shower. "Ready to get started?"

Phoenix grimaced, then replied, "No pain, no gain!"

"That's right, Mr. C." Adam's gaze shifted to Sierra. "I thought we'd start with some stretching exercises and then move on to the strengthening ones. But eventually, we'll need to use the equipment in your room."

"Of course. That won't be a problem." She sent Phoenix an encouraging smile. "Good luck!"

Around noon that day, Phoenix made his way to the dining room. He was tired and sore from his therapy session, but he refused to lie down. Not only because he'd promised Adam but because Sierra had said she'd join him for lunch.

"Phoenix Chamberlain, is that you?" a familiar voice cried out.

He turned to find Monica Swarovski crossing the floor to his table. At one time the two of them had dated. Not surprisingly, Monica had wanted to get married. Phoenix, meanwhile, had wanted to defy death on the slopes. She had been a vivacious, black-haired beauty. Even so, he had no regrets.

When Monica reached his table, he tried to stand.

"Oh no, don't get up." She pressed her perfectly manicured hand to his shoulder and then leaned down to kiss his cheek. "I ran into your mother and father at the country club."

Before she could say anything else, he corrected her. "My stepfather."

"Anyway, she told me that you were here." Monica's tone turned sweet with empathy. "How are you dear?"

"I'm fine," he answered, offering a patronizing smile.

"I've been worried about you, Phoenix. If there's anything I can do for you, just ask." She leaned in closer, showing off her cleavage, and said barely above a whisper, "I never got over you."

Just as Monica made her confession, Sierra walked up to the table. With one brow arched, her gaze slid from Phoenix to the woman standing there. "Should I get another chair?" she asked.

Monica peered at her, noticing the resort's logo on her shirt, and replied, "The table already has two chairs."

"Yes, but they're both taken," Sierra stated as she dropped into the vacant chair.

Monica transferred her outraged glare from Sierra to Phoenix. Not sure what to say, he made introductions. "Sierra Ramstad, this is *Mrs.* Monica Swarovski," adding an emphasis on the Mrs. "Monica, Sierra."

"Sierra, I see that you work here." Monica's tone was condescending. "Phoenix and I dated and we're still very close," she added.

"That's nice," Sierra quipped, using the same mocking tone.

Monica's eyes narrowed. "Phoenix and I were having a private conversation. If you will excuse yourself."

"Shall I leave?" Sierra asked him.

"No, we had a lunch date." He shifted his gaze to Monica. "My days on the slopes are over, he stated," surprised by the absence of bitterness. "But there's really no need for your concern."

"Oh, Phoenix," Monica wailed, her tone dry.

"Shall I leave you two alone?" Sierra asked again.

"There's no need. Monica won't be staying." He returned his gaze back to the dark-haired raven.

She pursed her lips together and nodded. "If you need me, you know how to reach me." She shot Sierra a pointed look before leaning over to kiss Phoenix on the cheek. Then she turned to leave.

Sierra smiled. She seemed content, happy. To him, she was beautiful, and growing more so with each new day. For the first time in his life, Phoenix was falling in love.

The cane Sierra had ordered online for Phoenix had finally arrived. It was black with an ornately carved handle inlaid with mother-of-pearl. It had character, unlike the replacement Adam had purchased at a local drugstore.

"I have a surprise for you," she told him.

His gaze lingered on her mouth. "A surprise," he quipped with a grin.

"I just need to make a quick call," she said, ringing Adam from her cell. He answered immediately since he'd been expecting her call.

"Now." That was all Sierra said before hanging up.

"Very cryptic," Phoenix murmured. "You definitely have me intrigued."

He changed his tone as soon as Adam came in carrying the cane. "I wonder what it could be," he said dryly as he took the cane from Adam, who turned to walk away.

Phoenix glanced over at her then. "Thank you," he replied with feeling.

Chapter Ten

"Going for your walk?" Phoenix asked the following evening as Sierra laced up her shoes. She had changed into shorts and he took the opportunity to admire her toned legs.

"That's right. I won't be gone long."

Since their lunch the day before, Phoenix hadn't had a moment alone with her. Adam was always with them on the deck in the mornings and he was in the room with them now. Three had definitely become a crowd.

"Do you mind if I go with you?'

Sierra blinked in surprise. "For a walk on the beach?"

"Isn't that where you walk?" he asked slowly.

She looked over at Adam.

In exasperation, Phoenix asked, "Do I need to get his permission?"

"No, I just wanted to be sure that Adam thought it was a good idea."

"You had a pretty intense workout earlier. Are you sure you're up to it, boss?" asked his physical therapist.

The only thing Phoenix was sure of was that he wanted some time alone with Sierra. He smiled and nodded. "I'm sure."

Sierra walked close by his side as they made their way to the beach. Even though they walked on a well-worn path between the dunes, the progress was slow. Once they were on the beach, she pointed to where the surf crashed onto the shore. "It will be easier if we walk down there."

Once they reached the compacted, damp sand, walking was indeed much easier. Sierra skipped around to avoid the waves that lapped ashore in their path. Phoenix, however, had neither the agility nor the coordination to do so, which meant his feet and pants were soon wet. But he didn't care.

"You're doing well," she commented.

"Thanks. I'm trying not to embarrass myself in front you." He reached for her hand and stopped walking, forcing her to as well. He was tempted to kiss her but he had something to say.

"I know the kind of reputation I have."

Her lips quirked with humor. "So do I. I read the stories."

"And?" he prompted.

"Where there's smoke there's fire," she replied her tone wry.

A full-fledged blaze in his case, Phoenix thought. He'd lived carelessly, surrounded by people as adrift, and unambitious as he was. "Let me guess," he began. "You believe I was a playboy, living off my trust fund, partying seven days a week."

As he spoke, the water frothed around their ankles before receding. Sierra didn't try to avoid it this time. He had her complete attention. He watched her closely and tried to gauge her reaction.

"Was I wrong?" she asked.

"No, not in the least." It was a hard thing to admit to her, yet the admission was liberating at the same time. "I'm not proud of it, but I was all of those things."

"Was?" she quizzed and squeezed his hand.

"I have changed, Sierra. I want to be sure that you know that."

She studied his face, wide green eyes unblinking.

His emotions were churning as forcefully as the surf. "I've never met anyone quite like you."

"Oh, really?"

His heart sank. It wasn't exactly what he'd hoped to hear. He lowered his head, his tone beseeching as he pressed, "I thought you felt...something for me."

"You're my boss, Phoenix."

"What if I wasn't?" he rationalized. So much was in flux, including his emotions. "Tell me you're not attracted to me."

She managed a strangled laugh. "That's not fair. You know that I'm attracted to you. I'm just not sure that I'm interested in a relationship."

Phoenix wasn't sure he was either. But he suspected her reasons were not quite as shallow as his. "Your ex-husband must have hurt you pretty bad."

"He did." The words came out so softly Phoenix was barely able to hear them.

"Do you want to talk about it?" he asked. Sierra's eyes widened with surprise. He chuckled drily. "I think I've become a better listener over the past few weeks."

The evolution of Phoenix Chamberlain continued, he marveled. And the woman beside him had played a huge role in his personal growth.

"I don't like to think about it, much less talk about it," she replied.

"Sure. I understand." He nodded as they started to walk again, their fingers still loosely woven together.

"Turner was a cop. A good friend of my sister's husband, Del. That's how we met. We had a whirlwind relationship…"

When she paused, Phoenix couldn't help but ask, "What happened?"

"You know I've asked myself that question a hundred times." Sierra frowned. "All I know is the solicitous man I dated and the one I married were like Dr. Jekyll and Mr. Hyde."

Phoenix gripped his cane with a little more force. "Did he hurt you?"

"Yes." It took her a moment to go on. In that time Phoenix's blood ran cold.

"Physically, mentally…emotionally," she admitted. Hand in hand they continued to walk and she went on with what he knew had to be a painful recitation of her past.

"The bruises faded so it was easier to get past the physical damage. But it has taken me longer to deal with the mental and emotional abuse."

Phoenix nodded but didn't say anything right away. They had both suffered devastating injuries, he realized, albeit in different ways. Hers had been inflicted on her psyche. His were physical and more obvious, but that didn't make them more debilitating.

"Sounds as if you could write a book," Phoenix said, trying to keep the conversation light even though he wanted to wrap his hands around her ex-husband's throat.

She sent him an amusing look. "I have entertained the thought."

Something occurred to Phoenix at that moment. "Does he know where you are?"

"I'm not in some kind of Witness Protection Program," she replied somewhat indignantly.

He sent her a smile, giving her time to continue if she wanted to.

She exhaled a deep breath. "That's my story. Are you sorry that you asked?"

"No." And he wasn't. "I am sorry that you had to go through all of that."

"Ready to turn around and head back to the resort?" she quizzed.

"Let's walk a little farther," he replied.

Phoenix was tired, but Sierra inspired him. Faced with adversity, she could have given up, but she hadn't. And he wasn't either. More than ever, he felt as if he something to prove to both of them.

Chapter Eleven

Phoenix certainly had undergone a transformation since his arrival in Seaside more than two months earlier. It was well into summer now, the heat outside almost intolerable even with the ocean's breeze. But he hadn't used that as an excuse to ease up on his rehabilitation efforts. Despite his grueling daily workouts with Adam, he walked on the beach with Sierra each evening.

Even more noticeable than his physical transformation were his emotional and spiritual ones. He appeared to have discovered a sense of purpose and seemed at peace with his situation. During the day, he could be found out and about in the resort, greeting guests or fraternizing with his employees.

And he'd won over Sierra; despite what she'd told him about not being in the market for a relationship. But what the future held for them was unclear.

Phoenix was getting stronger every day. That was the outcome she'd often prayed for when he'd first arrived because she was eager to see him leave. But now he seemed to be as connected to the resort as she was and she wondered if it was enough for him to stay?

She glanced up to find Phoenix standing in the doorway of her office. She hadn't heard his approach, partly because he no longer dragged his foot when he walked, but more so because she had been so preoccupied.

He was tanned from time spent outdoors and he wore a lopsided grin where the corners of his mouth used to be turned down with pain. Even though he hadn't had his hair cut since his arrival, he was ridiculously handsome. And the long hair gave him a bad boy vibe that Sierra couldn't resist.

"I'd like to take you out to dinner," he announced.

"Really?" she asked slowly.

"Yes. But this isn't business related, Sierra. So, I'll understand if you say no." He sobered.

Her heart did a somersault. She was nervous, although something had been brewing between them since that first kiss. But it had been easier to marginalize those feelings with the confinement of their professional relationship. Now he was making it clear that he wanted something more. As his employee, she urged herself to say no. But as a woman who found Phoenix attractive and intriguing, she wanted to say yes. And so she did.

Sierra had almost forgotten what it was like to get dressed up to go on a date. She'd decided on a simple black dress and conservative three inch heels. Both were a few years old and she could only hope that they were still in style. She put on a pair of insignificant diamond earrings and sprayed on her favorite perfume. Her sister called as Sierra studied her reflection in the mirror.

"I can't talk right now," she told Sienna almost immediately.

"It's Friday night. You should go out and kick up your heels once in a while."

Sierra hadn't told her family of her and Phoenix's relationship because she hadn't been sure where it was headed. Not to mention, Phoenix's picture was probably in the dictionary beside the word *womanizer*. Still, she valued her sister's opinion and let out the truth in a rush of words. "Phoenix and I are going out tonight."

"On a date?" Sienna quizzed.

Sierra took a deep breath and exhaled. "Yes, I am getting ready right now."

"Are you nervous?" her sister asked.

"A little," she replied as she examined her reflection. Her eyes were her best feature and she'd added more eye liner and mascara than usual. "Phoenix and I have been spending a lot of time together," she added.

"Enjoy yourself, sis. I'm just surprised, that's all. You haven't breathed a word of it to me," Sienna shot back.

"I'm sorry. I'm not sure what my feelings are, or his." She fussed with her hair, which she had put up for the occasion. "Whatever happens between Phoenix and me, I'm not going to romanticize it."

From the hallway, she heard the tap-tap of Phoenix's cane. Excitement bubbled up, breaking her outward calm. "I've got to go. We'll talk about this another time."

"Do you promise?" Sienna quizzed.

"Yes, I promise."

Then Sierra hung up the phone and opened the door. Despite all of her talk about not romanticizing her relationship with Phoenix, one look at his handsome face and she was lost.

Sierra stood in the doorway, a vision of beauty in a delicate black dress that hugged her curvaceous body. Phoenix's heart fluttered the same way it used to whenever he'd stood at the top of a ski slope gazing down. "You look amazing," he told her.

"Thank you." She smiled as she fussed with her hair. "You look great too."

He glanced down at the silk suit and tie he was wearing. "I forgot what it is like to wear something other than track pants and t-shirts."

"I wondered where you would wear all of the clothes that you brought with you," she admitted.

"I'm glad I did so I have something to wear for our date," he told her. She had accepted Phoenix despite his scars and disability or maybe because of them. She was an extraordinary woman and he wanted to impress her, to dazzle her. If that made him shallow, then so be it.

"We have reservations," he announced. He had made plans that included a sumptuous meal at Makati's steakhouse and a champagne toast to the beginning of what he hoped would be a long, happy relationship.

His plans were forgotten the moment their lips touched. Vaguely, he was aware of his cane falling to the floor, as his hands made their way to her waist and their mouths fused together. "Perhaps we should go now," she said softly, the words coming out between panting breaths.

"Yes, you're probably right." he admitted. His smile was every bit as cunning.

Tommy was sitting in the lobby when Phoenix and Sierra entered the room. He pushed to his feet. "Are you two ready to go?"

"Yes," Phoenix replied.

The driver nodded. "I'll bring the Cadillac around and we'll be on our way."

Although they were late for their reservations at Makati's, a hundred dollar bill handed to the maître d' apparently smoothed over any misunderstandings. The upscale restaurant was located in a newly renovated two story building. The first floor was open to all diners. The second where they were seated, was reserved for A-list guests.

As soon as they were seated at their table, a black-vested server arrived with a silver tray carrying two champagne flutes and a bottle of Dom Perignon. "Shall I pour?" he asked Phoenix.

"Yes, please," he replied.

Phoenix was accustomed to the royal treatment. She was dazzled by his lifestyle, but she realized it represented a world she knew little about; a world to which he would be returning in the not-so-distant future.

"Enjoy," the waiter said before turning to leave.

Once they were alone again, Phoenix raised his glass and said, "To you."

Sierra clanked the rim of her champagne flute against his. "To us."

Chapter Twelve

Only one week of the summer season remained. Once the Labor Day holiday passed, the town would be quieter and the resort a little slower until the snowbirds started arriving in October. Sierra was looking forward to taking some time off to spend it with Phoenix.

The past couple of weeks had been a blur of stolen moments during the day and walks on the beach in the evenings. The depth of her feelings surprised her. Falling in love with her boss hadn't been her intention, but that was what had happened. Even though he hadn't said so, she was certain Phoenix felt the same way. His touch and passionate kisses told her so.

It was seven o'clock, and Phoenix was already up and dressed. Just as she'd learned to be spontaneous, Sierra had learned to appreciate surprises. Yesterday, he had surprised her with bouquet of a dozen long-stemmed red roses. They were in a crystal vase on her desk, their fragrance perfuming the air.

And a few days earlier, he had invited his mother and stepfather to come to the resort for a visit. Sierra had assumed he wanted to begin restoring their relationship and she'd been proud of him for extending the invitation. Pride had morphed into shock when he'd introduced her to them as his girlfriend rather than as the resort's manager. She smiled at the memory.

"What's taking you so long?" she called out for Phoenix.

"Perfection takes time," he replied from down the hall.

"All I need is you!" she exclaimed as she threw her arms open wide, connecting with the vase of flowers. The vase of roses tumbled to the floor, spilling water over the hardwood. "Oh no!" she cried out.

Sierra opened one of the desk drawers, where she kept a box of tissues. A manila envelope, with her name printed on it, caught her attention. She hadn't put it there which could only mean that Phoenix had. But what was it? She reached for it and opened the flap. The roses were forgotten as she stared at the document she'd pulled from inside the envelope. She swallowed in disbelief and her heart broke as she read Phoenix's plan to dismiss her.

Minutes later, Phoenix filled the doorway and called, "Surprise!"

He held a tray laden with breakfast and two cups of coffee. As distraught as she was, it barely registered that he was standing without his cane. The only thing Sierra was focused on was the ache in her chest.

Indeed she was surprised. All this time she'd been worrying about where their burgeoning relationship was heading, it had never occurred to her that he might ask her to leave.

"When were you going to spring this surprise on me?" she asked coldly.

Phoenix blinked in confusion. His face reddened and a guilty grimace replaced his smile. "Where did you get that?" he asked.

"It was in the desk. I opened it because it was addressed to me."

"Sierra, it's not what it looks like." He limped into the room, sloshing coffee over the rim of the cups, and set the tray on her desk.

"You're a liar and a manipulator!" she yelled.

"Yes…I mean no!" he stammered. "When I came back, my plans were to take over the resort once I had recuperated. I didn't think you'd want to stay, but I'd planned to give you a choice."

"How nice of you to give me options," she snarled.

"I know it looks bad, but I had this drawn up months ago. Before you and I…"

"What?" she asked flatly.

"Fell in love," he insisted.

But she wouldn't hear it. She couldn't believe what was happening. Her eyes blurred with tears as she studied the document. "You're very generous, by the way. I've been well compensated for my…*service*." Her stomach hurled on the last word. She felt used. And stupid, because she'd fallen in love with Phoenix and she should have known better.

Sierra fled from the office, not stopping when he called her name. She couldn't stay here now. She was at the lobby door, fingers curled around the doorknob when she heard a crash followed by an ensuing sob. She turned and walked back through the lobby and looked down the hallway. Phoenix was lying face down on the floor just outside of the office.

"Phoenix!" she cried out.

He raised his head. His face was damp. He was crying.

"Are you okay," she asked.

He pushed himself up so that he was in a sitting position with his back against the wall. "No, I'm not okay, Sierra!"

"I'll get Adam."

Before she could turn to leave, Phoenix grabbed her by the hand. "I don't need Adam, I need you."

She swallowed hard. He'd never told her that before. "You were going to let me go."

"Yes, but Sierra…" Phoenix closed his eyes and let his hand drop to his side. "I changed my mind."

"How could you forget something like this?" she demanded, shaking the envelope of papers in front of his face.

"You made me forget a lot of things," Phoenix stated. "You taught me to believe in myself. How to accept my life as it was and to embrace the future." He paused. "I love you."

I love you. The words snatched her breath away. She had been in love before. And her ex-husband had used the word but mangled its meaning. How could she trust Phoenix and love again? How different was this man from the brooding and broken man who'd first arrived and turned her life upside down with his edicts and demands.

"Do you really love me?" She whispered the words as she dropped down beside him on the floor.

"Yes, more and more with each day that passes," Phoenix replied, reaching for her. "I'm sorry. Please tell me that you'll stay here with me. I want Seaside Haven to be our home."

Sierra framed his face with her hands, kissing his damp cheek. Just before their mouths met, she whispered, "I love you, too."

www.ingramcontent.com/pod-product-compliance
Lightning Source LLC
Chambersburg PA
CBHW030427310726
48979CB00009B/1657/J

* 9 7 8 1 3 2 9 0 1 5 7 8 4 *